The Space Adventures of
Kirk Sandblaster
Space Adventurer

Also by Oli Jacobs:

Filmic Cuts 1: Sunshine & Lollipops
Filmic Cuts 2: Luchador Monkey Crisis
Filmic Cuts 3: Curse of the Ellipsis...
The Station 17 Chronicles
(Underneath/Stains)
Kirk Sandblaster and the Ice Pirates of Llurr
Bad Sandwich
Strange Days in High Wycombe

For you, you lucky thing you...

Copyright Oli Jacobs 2012
Second Edition
ISBN: 978-1-291-31609-4

Artwork by CM Carter (@BreakfastChamp)
http://www.breakfastchampion.com

The Space Adventures of Kirk Sandblaster: Space Adventurer

By
Oli Jacobs

1

Against the deep, dark blackness of the Dilure Quadrant, several tiny stars shone brightly like little candles celebrating a very old birthday. Some were still, twinkling against the vast emptiness that housed them, while others zoomed and raced light years away. Some would look out on this sight and feel at peace, in awe of the wonder of it all. They'd marvel at the possibilities that the stars would represent, and the sheer size of the Universe that held them.

To a tiny Ctolian like Pikpik, it was just an irritating reminder of his failures.

He had been a star-miner, part of an elite group who travelled to the stars that shone brightest. They discovered the suns that lay behind the glow, excavating them for precious resources that could go to anyone from energy barons to jewellers. It was a sweet gig, and one that Pikpik did very well. Until he got laid off.

"Budget reasons" was their explanation, but after drowning his sorrow with Xubton Juices he returned to his modest Space-Villa to find his boss in, well, "relations" with Pikpik's wife.

Since then Pikpik had been travelling the Dilure Quadrant with nothing but his tiny vessel and a few meagre belongings. As a Ctolian, he was mere inches in height to a Human eye and looking much a squashed turtle; looks which couldn't compete with his boss's Horgorian ancestry. All muscles and hair and... size. But his tiny stature meant he could travel the Universe, un-noticed and un-bothered, giving Pikpik time to let off steam and make plans for his new future.

But each star, each shining beacon of beauty, made him even madder.

He was determined to turn back and show his boss what a Ctolian was capable of. True they, as a species, had never been in combat. Rather, they were mostly being blown away by massive gusts of wind. But he'd seen many Holo-Shows, and picked up a few tricks. Yes, Pikpik would turn his vessel around, take back his wife, claim his Space-Villa and, glat it, take that big Horgorian's job to boot!

He would have, if when he turned around his vessel, he hadn't run into a much larger ship that punted him halfway across the Quadrant.

The ship in question was The Bounty, a ramshackle Frankenstein's Monster of a spacecraft that wouldn't even get 30 Tetras in this Universe. Only a fool would buy one, and only a bigger fool would fly it at such speeds that it's panels would flicker with the threat of disintegration, leaving behind a skeletal structure in the Big Empty known as space.

Inside, the fool in question was Kirk Sandblaster, and the bigger fool pushing The Bounty to the limit was his sidekick-come-partner, Xlaar.

And behind them, the reason they were pushing this craft to a dangerous level of speed and pressure, was a fleet of Ghurian plunderers, whose use of lasers and electrolyzers showed a certain lack of delight.

Looking at The Bounty's rear monitor, Kirk Sandblaster smirked.

"Looks like they're giving up!"

Sandblaster was a human, in the middle of his 30th year and with all the gusto that that provided. He slicked his slight quiff to one side and took a seat back in a chair, humbly labelled CAPTAIN.

"You need an extra pair of eyes!" Xlaar growled, frantically working at the controls with each of his four arms.

"That's why I have you!"

Xlaar was a Zaarian, a race of lizard-like creatures blessed with two heads and four arms. To compliment their weak, slender frames, they often dressed in muscular powersuits, with Xlaar's crimson one suggesting a high rank within his particular tribe.

Right now though, he was pretty far from home and doing all the work while his cocky comrade popped open a bottle of Cartereli Ale and put his chair in recline.

"I think some music would go down well right now, don't you?"

"How about you give me some glatting help!"

"Why? We're fine! You saw their ships ease off..."

"In my experience there's usually a reason for that!"

"Pfft, relax... I'm sure nothing will go..."

Before Sandblaster could finish, a bright fire passed through The Bounty's cockpit window. All six eyes of its crew looked out as something glistened the black with a burning arc, curving wonderfully before them.

"Would that be your reason?" Sandblaster asked.

Both Xlaar's heads nodded.

The creator of the fiery arc was a Xdian Trailblazer Missile, and its trail was blazing towards The Bounty.

Xlaar immediately threw all hands on the controls and contorted the ship quickly enough so that the missile flew past. But it was not enough. It was locked on and ready to quickly transform The Bounty into several tiny pieces if they didn't do something. In between losing his footing with Xlaar's crazed steering, Sandblaster had a Eureka moment.

"I have a plan!"

"Does it involve helping me steer?"

"No."

"Then forgive me if I start getting nervous!"

"Don't be, it's a phenomenal plan!"

With that, Sandblaster jumped up and ran to the rear of the ship. Xlaar shouted in confusion behind him as the Trailblazer flew past again and made a nice little looping effect before missing once more.

Just.

Sandblaster entered the ship's rear dock, still filled with various knick-knacks and junk that he'd been too lazy to remove. Not that he'd admit that to Xlaar, instead saying that it was "all part of the plan". But the plan was in its infancy, and not wholly guaranteed. He grabbed an O2 mask from the wall and attached himself to a pole on the wall. As The Bounty lurched around, Sandblaster moved various crates and piles of scrap towards the rear bay doors, and took a moment to look proudly upon his work.

The ship threw itself to the side again as Sandblaster heard a *whizz* outside.

"Time to take out the trash!" Sandblaster muttered, before looking sad that no one was around to hear his quip.

He reached across to the primitive controls for the bay doors, punched a few buttons and then took a deep breath of O2 as they opened to reveal the great black beyond. Instantly, the anonymous crates and various bits of metal flew out the back, floating idly behind them.

And just like he had planned, Sandblaster watched as the Trailblazer made one last burning turn, threw itself towards its target, and blew up against what looked like an old arcade machine.

The blast rocked the ship a little, but Sandblaster was pleased with what he saw, and punched the doors closed. However, what he hadn't noticed was that the impact of the explosion had dislodged the pole he was clinging to, and with the suck of space still fierce, it spun around and went to join the rest of the wreckage, taking Sandblaster with it.

Before he was completely taken outside, Sandblaster managed to grab hold of The Bounty's bay doors. They were shutting slowly, and jarred at points as the old hydraulics shuddered to life. As he desperately tried to pull himself in, Sandblaster looked out into the black and saw the Ghurians had caught up again, deftly knocking aside his man-made obstacle course.

Finally, as he felt the belt of his trousers start to give way, the doors reached where Sandblaster was holding on, and he managed to throw up a leg and climb back in. After a crunch of metal on metal, he fell to floor as normal gravity was restored.

As he re-entered the cockpit, Xlaar's right head looked at Sandblaster suspiciously.

"Nothing to it." Sandblaster shrugged.

"Yeah, anyway, they caught up! What now?"

"We out run them again. I mean it's not like they have another one of those missiles is it?"

A familiar *whizz* passed them in stereo as they looked out, seeing a rather wonderful looking double rainbow of burning pain arrive on the scene.

"No Kirk, they have TWO!"

Sandblaster stroked his chin and took stock as the missiles danced around menacingly in front of them.

"Maybe we should turn on Navi for help?"

Xlaar shot a glare of such intensity that only came with having four eyes. "Don't you dare turn on that pompous pile of..."

Sandblaster pressed a button, and a jaunty voice echoed through The Bounty.

"Well ring-a-ding and hello Dolly! What can I do for you fine adventurers today?"

"SHUT UP!" Xlaar responded.

"Navi, we have 2 trailblazers looking to knock us out the sky, any suggestions?"

"Well sure as Shirley I can tell you that! Just need to make a few calculations! Anything else while I dot the i's?"

Xlaar shook his heads scornfully. "Yeah, how did we end up in this mess?"

"Good question! It all started in Earth Year 2012..."

In a moment, Sandblaster and Xlaar looked at each other, realizing what they'd just done.

"NOOOO!"

2

Back in the shiny days of the year 2012, Earth had regained its spirit of adventure. In the very, very past, it had looked to the skies and thought to itself, "Yes, I want a piece of that." So they threw dogs and monkeys and the odd Austrian up into the stratosphere to see what they would find. More often than not, it was simply more space.

Although the dogs did have a good root around. They had a motto you see: There's No Bones Like Space Bones.

There never were any space bones.

But eventually man himself decided to venture out into the big black divide. This, of course, was before the Gender Wars of 2069 that saw a Female Uprising take control of the Earth's powers. But to be fair, the Men were all glad of the change anyway.

But back to the beginning of this chain of events. Man flew up to the skies and beyond, and after many tentative steps finally put their boot-print on the first port of call: The Moon (or as it's known now, Armstrongville). There they placed their flags and gave themselves a mighty pat on the back. They had reached into the stars and made themselves at home.

But then... nothing. Not a jot. The occasional chin-stroke at what could be done further but no real drive to do it. It was a bit of a celestial rut.

But then a plucky little robot was chosen to go to the next stage of discovery: Mars. There man's curiosity would be sated in the form of a tiny bot known, naturally, as Curiosity. He would trundle along, looking at the red planet in all its rocky forms. Days passed, then weeks and months, and the people below were perfectly content with their interesting rocks and various mineral deposits.

That was until one day, when the Martians decided to say "Hello" in the form of a collection of rocks and Curiosity's own manipulated camera.

It was the first First Contact, and naturally the human race was very scared. Years of ancient digi-reels had told them stories of invading Martians with big green heads and a hatred for Tom Jones. But in reality the Martians were a simple race. Nano in size but with a technological intellect stretching across the galaxy. They had been viewing us for years in their tiny ships, but had thought us a hostile race when being swatted out the sky or sprayed with chemicals from cans. Luckily for us the Martians were quite docile, and took the whole thing as a harmless misunderstanding.

The two races began communicating almost immediately, with the Earth folk eager to learn all that the Martians had to tell. Everything from interstellar travel to the secrets of the universe was passed on, whetting Earth's appetite for discovery even further. The first foundations of what would see years of space travel were laid, everything from Quantum Cores to those little rubber balls that seem to bounce around and not really do anything but are actually quite important.

However, Earth's penchant for destruction reared its ugly head, and Man craved knowledge of how to improve their arms. If they were to reach out beyond their galaxy into the far-flung recesses of space, they had to be ready for any hostile forces. The Martians understood, and offered to fine-tune all of Earth's weapons. Countries came together in the hopes of having bigger and better weapons than the other, offering the Martians everything they could offer. From the hungry West, to the secretive East, all leaders across Earth came to the Martians to help build the strongest forces. Space Travel could wait, now they had Space Weapons.

So naturally, when the Martians allowed everyone's weapons to be tried out, they soon discovered that all their nuclear bombs, rapid-fire artillery and hulking tanks were reduced to nothing more than scrap. The Martian technology had muted every offensive weapon from all corners of the globe. Ray Guns turned into harmless tanning devices, nuclear capabilities instead safely powered small music boxes. Normally the Earth folk would simply return back to their bullets and booms, but they had all scrapped those in fervour over the Martian technology.

When questioned, the Martians played dumb, and instead the Great Peace was announced instead, with all nations of the Earth deciding to return to Space Adventuring rather than mess with these Martian pacifists. Seriously, those guys were just plain weird.

"GET TO THE GLATTING POINT!" Roared Xlaar, all four arms racing around the controls.

Sandblaster was mid-way through a sandwich as the reality of explosions and sirens and general space stress came back to him. He had got so into Navi's stories that he had forgotten about all the potential destruction and kidnapping by Ghurian plunderers. Still...

"I'm sure we have time for Navi to finish..."

"WE'RE UNDER ATTACK!"

"Good point." Sandblaster chomped down the remains of his sandwich and sat forward, puffing out his chest and getting in full-on captain mode.

"Navi, give me the York Notes version of the rest of the events."

"Sure and dandy days!"

As Sandblaster sat back in his chair, Xlaar performed the mightiest face-palm ever seen in the Quadrants. If the Grand Recordists had been around, they would have pointed out its clever use of all four of his hands across both his faces, in addition to the current combat conditions they were under.

As Sandblaster considered another sandwich, for they were very tasty, Navi continued.

"Now where the dumb-dumb devil was I? Oh yes! The Newniverse..."

Once the Great Peace was implemented on Earth, the wonders of the galaxy were unlocked for them to explore. There, the noble Humans encountered many strange and exotic beings and species, all of which had been touched by the tinkering hands of the Martians. Therefore, they had also lost any semblance of violent intent and instead any aggravated behaviour was usually just done with stern looks and mad flailing of the arms. In some instances, this worked in scaring the Humans.

However, history was not built on running away. It was built on war and plunder, grit and determination. But seeing as the Great Peace swept across the newly discovered Quadrants like a rather nasty Flexian Flu, the likes of the Humans did the next best thing.

They bought about a system of government.

Over the course of a few decades, the galactic government known as Universia was established. Featuring beings from across all edges of space, and sometimes time, it was the hub for all new, exciting things like diplomacy, commerce and tiny, tiny pens. Naturally, there were some planets that were a little miffed at the fact that their happy little homes may be turned into mining colonies. All thanks, of course, to the mass vote of a few beings that existed several Quadrants across the galaxy. Their collars, and other strange parts, were ruffled, and so they would declare war.

Naturally, this was a pointless act as nobody could really kill anyone. All weapons now merely stunned or made you feel a bit sore, but nothing that would require a procession.

But still, some beings would declare war and do terrible things like inconveniencing the Universia government with needless red tape, or causing transport routes to get blocked or trade to be lost and, invariably, go off. Such acts of sabotage caused Universia to implement the Galactic Army Force, or GAF for short.

The Humans found this very funny. Others, such as the Zaarians, didn't quite get the joke.

The Galactic Army Force ran their ships across the blackness of space, taking on any being or beast that opposed the law of Universia. Bruises were dished out and nasty fines were placed for any behaviour deemed "bad". The most famous of wars was the Great Battle of Halack, which lasted for several hours and caused some forces on both sides not to get a proper nights sleep.

As you can imagine, there were some seriously narked casualties in that conflict.

However, while any wars were quick and to the point, there was one area of space that even the GAF feared to tread. Universia dubbed it the "Dark Quadrant", an unexplored section of space that was so-called due to the fact that no star shone there, and any ships that entered never returned. Some GAF forces were sent one day to investigate, full of the best of the best and stocked to the brim with the finest defences. Of the three ships, two entered and were never seen again.

The third got to the edge of the Dark Quadrant, and then promptly stopped, where some observers note that a tiny escape pod popped out the side and flew off, far away from the Dark Quadrant.

When the crew of this third ship were questioned as to why they stopped, they merely said they were following orders. When asked who from, the answer was the same as the question "And which foolish coward blasted himself out into space and from the GAF, and into the history books of disgrace?"

One name.

Kirk. Sandblaster.

Sandblaster smiled from his seated position and looked up at Xlaar.

"Hey that's me!"

Xlaar gave him the nastiest look that all four of his eyes could give. Sandblaster looked a bit hurt by the lack of enthusiasm his co-pilot showed.

"You just don't appreciate a good yarn." He said, as a massive explosion boomed outside and shook their ship like a cocktail mixer at a classy bar.

Talking of which, Navi continued his story, to Sandblaster's great delight...

On the terraformed planet of Frexia, only lowlifes and vagabonds reside. While most planets had flourished due to the massive amount of Tetras, the agreed upon universal currency, that tourism from other beings had bought, Frexia had chosen the less-wise resources. Primarily, mind-spirits, chance games and... well, ask your father. He might know the rest.

Anyway, within this particular district, in this particular terraform zone on Frexia known as Terraform 43, there was a bar that had a notorious reputation across the planetary systems. The Paxion Arms, a mind-spirit joint signified by its logo featuring a rather delightful female with many arms and many...

Seriously, ask your dad. We're not getting into this.

The Paxion Arms greeted its visitors with the bright lights and garish symbols that only the finest drink joints could offer. It was all class, as long as the person visiting had a sliding scale of what they considered class to actually be. But in the hive of dirty browns and gunmetal greys of Terraform 43, it was an oasis. Albeit one full with intoxicating liquids.

The bar's owner, a grizzled Cy-Man called Marec, kept the Paxion Arms as tight as any ship he had served under. Once, Marec had been a Human under the employ of the GAF, one that was firm of body and mind. He rose strategically through the ranks, from the lowliest slop-boy to the commander of one of the greatest vessels known to man: the Epic.

However after one particularly gruelling battle against Ghurian pirates, Marec had celebrated too hard with many a mind-spirit, and ended up crashing the Epic, a ship the size of a minor planet, into a minor planet. Pellian VII to be exact. Luckily the Pellians didn't care for VII, being more fans of Pellians II-VI. Plus the cataclysmic implosion caused the creation of Pellian VIII and IX, which are very popular holiday destinations till this day.

Marec though was less lucky, losing most of his facilities and his collected ranks. Therefore here he was, using the last of his GAF pension to fit himself with the finest cybernetic prosthetics courtesy of BOTECHNIQUE ULTRA! THE FINEST IN ROBO-CY-MECHA-BOT-TRON ENHANCEMENTS! DON'T DELAY WITH YOUR WEAK BIOLOGICAL PIECES! BUY A BOTECHNIQUE ENHANCEMENT TODAY!

Both Sandblaster and Xlaar looked curious at Navi for a moment. Even the Ghurian pirates, who had stopped their volley of sidewinders to listen in to the story via hacked comms, were confused.

"Gee I'm sorry about that folks!" Navi explained, "That darn advertising just plum gets in everywhere!"

Everyone nodded together in agreement, and went back to listening to the story.

At this particular time, the Paxion Arms was home to a few old dogs of the GAF. Seasoned veterans, who had served for years under the orders of Universia in keeping the galaxy in check, but had failed to take advantage of the finance plans they had offered. Therefore instead of sunning themselves on one of the many Solar Resorts around the Quadrants, they mingled in bars like these, piecing together what little Tetras they had left to get a gallon of mind-spirits and the company of... a friend. Just a friend. To talk. Nothing else.

On this occasion, one hardened ex-GAF named Bub was sat at the bar, nursing his way through a particularly potent brew of mind-spirit called Elejian Waft, a flouncy drink that no doubt hit the spot. Besides, if anybody questioned his choice then Bub would grab them by the nearest piece of flesh and throw them across the bar. Many years service under the GAF had made him bitter and jaded, and he now spent his evenings wondering "what if?" What if he had chosen a life of domesticity instead of adventure? What if he had raised a family, taken holidays on far off planets? What if he hadn't put all his Tetras into the doomed sport of Mind Chess, which was quite boring as mostly involved beings staring at each other and then one being declared the victor.

Bub thought all these things and more, but just found solace in the relative peace and quiet of the Paxion Arms and his flaggard of Waft. He even began to think that after all these years, all his bitterness and anger was drifting away. That he was finally beginning to find some sort of inner peace.

"Bar keep! One of your finest Cartereli Ales!"

But then, life has a nasty habit of poking you in the ribs when you're about to fall asleep.

All at once, Bub felt several years of cynicism, aggression, vitriol and pure-blind fury rise up in him. His eyes became wide, his nostrils flared like a solar explosion, and his blood boiled hotter than the hot tubs of Mercury.

Without even looking to where the voice came from, he began to growl.

"Only one man drinks such an old time drink. And that one man was a heathen and a coward who abandoned his comrades!"

Bub looked over, and sure enough standing there with enough aplomb to dazzle a black hole, was Kirk Sandblaster.

"I'll take two of those, but the coward bit is *not* my slice of jam."

Sandblaster was one of those unique sorts...

"Excellent! Me! My favourite part of all stories..."

"SHUT UP!" Xlaar and the Ghurians said in unison.

As I was saying... Sandblaster was one of those unique sorts that you only hear about in stories such as these. Impossibly youthful in looks, but old enough to know better, and with a stance that said "Hey there, that's right, it's me." The Grand Recordists called them "rogues", but most people saw them as either "idiots" or "irritants". Most found themselves blasted off into the deepest, most lonely areas of space, but Sandblaster seemed to have a luck and charm that kept him in the favour of whatever beings looked over all of us. Since the Dark Quadrant incident, he had carved a niche for both simultaneously being in trouble and keeping out of it. Something that blew the mind of most beings.

At times literally. Messy business...

But Bub wasn't taken in by his easy way and light attempts at conversation. He was ready to start a rumble.

"I note the GAF symbol on your shoulder, how's about a drink to celebrate our veteranship?" Kirk offered, a merry glint in his eye.

"I was on the ship that you blew yourself out of and left us to die!"

Sandblaster looked confused. He paid his Tetras and took a sip of his Cartereli.

"I'm pretty sure you wouldn't have died."

"We could have!"

"Well anybody could, figuratively, die. But all I did was leave you floating in space!"

Bub was knocked sideways by Sandblaster's casual revision of history. He remembered a death far worse than anything physical. A death of reputation, a death by a thousand cuts of a thousand words, mocking in tone. A death that he had never lived down to this day.

And now, a death he would pay back in kind.

"I'm going to KILL YOU SANDBLASTER!" Bub roared, lunging at his nemesis.

"I'm pretty sure you ca... NGH!"

Bub wrapped his old, wrinkled hands around Sandblaster's neck and looked him dead in the eye. Sandblaster was less interested in maintaining such intimate contact and more removing Bub's hands from his throat.

"Look... over there... something..."

"I'm not falling for that one!"

"Are... you sure? It's... very... interesting?"

Bub loosened his grip and turned to see where Sandblaster was pointing. All he saw was a wall, and while the decorative posters advertising various wares and activities *were* interesting, he didn't see how it corresponded to their fracas.

That was until Sandblaster threw his finely polished boot into Bub's groin and left the old man curled up on the floor, with a voice several octaves higher.

"And that, old man, is why I was a captain and you were a cook!"

"I was your third-in-command..." Bub squeaked.

"Oh. Well in that case, have another on me!"

Sandblaster laid some Tetras on the bar and met Marec's stern gaze with his best dazzling smile before leaving. After all, he hadn't time for reminiscing with vengeful shipmates from the GAF, he had bigger things on his mind.

Treasure!

Xlaar placed one of his many hands on Sandblaster's shoulder, nearly pulling him off his chair with his strength.

"If you betray me like that, I'll end you." He snarled.

Sandblaster nodded. "Duly noted."

Before they could carry on listening, a comms message came through the system. It was from the Ghurian ship chasing them. The two adventurers looked at each other before Sandblaster spun around and punched the button.

"What is it you space vagrants?"

"You has treasure?" The Ghurian whined, their voices very hard to listen to.

"Umm..."

"We was just chasing you for funs and that! Now we wants treasures!"

Sandblaster laughed and looked concerned at Xlaar, who had gone back to being amazed at the idiocy around him.

"Well, shall we see how the story goes first? I mean, we may *not* have the treasures?"

After a brief pause the Ghurians nasty vocals came through again.

"Trues. Tell compy thing to tell more story!"

Sandblaster spun back around and relaxed once more.

"You heard the pirate Navi, continue!"

4

While the shiny delights and wares of Terraform 43 were tempting for Kirk Sandblaster, and they were very tempting... with their shininess... oh so pretty...

Ahem.

After another hour of being tempted by the bright lights and verbose merchants, Sandblaster slapped himself about and focussed on the plan at hand. Rumours were abound that Frexia was home to a particular merchant who had a particular map that lead to a *very* particular treasure. A treasure that went beyond mere Tetras and shiny gems that were already around the planet. In brightly lit shops. Adorned with very reasonable prices...

With his last batch of Tetras exchanged for a few more bags of said gems, and the odd dash of mind-spirits, Sandblaster had words around Terraform 43's low lives. They were a veritable gallery of nogoodniks, out for a quick dash of cash or slither of delight. Sandblaster had none of those things to offer, but he did have his charm and bags of novelties...

"It's Ctolian jewels, worth millions!" He told one, curious ruffian. He... she... it was a Horgorian, several feet high and covered in fluff. If Sandblaster was to make this transaction, he needed his best glarp-eating grin.

The Horgorian took one of the gems, a shiny ruby-like stone, and eyed it up between his massive, chunky fingers.

"It's twice the size of a Ctolian." He bellowed.

"That's why they're so valuable in their culture!"

The Horgorian looked at it some more. "Wouldn't it crush them?"

"What's more precious than a jewel that could kill you?"

As the gem shined between his brutish digits, the Horgorian looked deep into its sparkling interior. However, as his eyes looked over the majesty of the stone, his fingers forgot their own strength, and reduced the gem to dust between his fingers.

Both Sandblaster and the Horgorian stood there in silence for a moment, as the gems dust rained beautifully down to the ground.

"I'll have to charge you for that." Sandblaster said, earning an irritated grunt from the beast before him.

Luckily, it was one beast that knew the honour of trade. It informed Sandblaster of who may be able to tell him more about this so-called "treasure"...

"What do you mean 'so-called'?"

Sandblaster sat up in his seat, taken with the sudden offence only a man of his valour could take from such a statement.

"Well sir, the proof is in the pudding and I'm afraid the pudding is not on the plate!" Navi told him.

"What in the name of Universia does that even mean?" Xlaar asked, tinkering away at the controls due to boredom at the whole mess.

"Now listen Navi, I have a map. A map I fought hard to get."

"Well we'll get toot-sweet to that soon sir-a-reeno! But righty-tighty now the treasure is just an assumption."

Sandblaster screwed his mouth up. He didn't like being sassed by a computer, much less one as annoying as Navi. Sure enough, after this the Ghurians rang through.

"No treasure?!?" The pirates bellowed, also a bit miffed at this turn of events.

"There's treasure! The man... thing... said so!"

"Computer says no!"

Sandblaster leaned into Navi's comms panel and gritted his teeth.

"Get on with the story and get to the part with the map." He said, making sure each word was intensely spelled out.

"Us's?"

"Oh! Um, no! I meant the computer."

"Ahs... make sense."

"I thought I did..."

"No! It make the sense!"

As the conversation went further downhill, Xlaar began wondering why he had left the possible worship he would have got on his home planet, for this farce. But then he remembered; the treasure.

With a mighty fist, the giant Zaarian bashed Navi and let the machine carry on with the tale.

Down one of the grimier areas of Terraform 43, where the currency was piles of dust and the values were even more fickle, Sandblaster walked along looking for the being that would lead him to possible riches. Or danger. If he was honest he was looking forward more to the latter. Several alien hobo's tried to persuade him to part with his reclaimed Tetras, thanks to a frugal use of returns policy, while others attempted to mug him for them. Alas, one beings efforts only resulted in an ineffective skin irritation, leaving both parties standing around rather awkwardly.

Once Sandblaster got to his destination he knew he was in the right place, thanks to the Horgorian telling him it would be labelled "G'Kay's Wares" and the sign saying the very same thing. He opened the rickety door and made his way in, preparing himself for what horrors lay waiting.

Sandblaster had no idea. G'Kay's Wares was some sort of bizarre pet shop, filled with creatures and critters from all corners of the Quadrants. Want an Earth dog? G'Kay had all breeds. A Ghurian Snapper Blight? Only the snappiest! Sandblaster even saw some cute little things that were banging the glass and shouting something like "we're not pets we're a species", but was distracted by a twee widdle rabbit instead.

He noted the titular trader, G'Kay, up ahead at the counter serving some brute from the outskirts of the Solaria Quadrant. When Earth had joined Universia, some enterprising humans had relocated to other planets in the hopes of a finer life. Some dabbled in eugenics. This massive behemoth looked to have chosen the Muscle Mass option only offered by the roid-crazed inhabitants of Rygan. His brawn was so enhanced he looked ready to pop. Compared to the Svakken G'Kay, a stooped, weaselly character, he was a skyscraper.

Sandblaster watched as the two bantered over one of those sweet little bunnies he had been mesmerised. Such little, fluffy things, with big eyes full of love. Sandblaster thought about maybe buying one himself to take on his adventures, use it to impress the females around the galaxy. Ladies loved cute bunnies, and so did Kirk Sandblaster.

His heart almost melted as he watched G'Kay pass the hulk one of the rabbits, with the brute seeming to fall instantly in love with its floppy ears and wide eyes. It was a beautiful scene, until the man hoisted the animal in the air, flicked it skywards, and gobbled it whole as it fell in his mouth. Sandblaster was stunned as the berserker paid his Tetras, and shoved his way past him.

"You see anything you like?"

Suddenly it all came falling into place. Sandblaster looked over at G'Kay, who was gesturing to a giant board listing all the creatures and their prices. All under the one word MENU.

This wasn't a pet shop. This was a fast food joint.

"I... I'm not hungry. Thanks."

"Then why you here?" G'Kay purred, his beady eyes lasering in on the rogue before him.

"I hear you have knowledge..."

"I have much knowledge."

"... of a treasure."

G'Kay grew silent and breathed noisily through his sharp teeth. He looked around his shop/restaurant-type place, before turning back to Sandblaster.

"Meet me round the back, and I'll tell you of your... treasure."

With that the Svakken scurried away, leaving Sandblaster standing there amongst a veritable menagerie of the galaxies breeds.

He was slightly miffed he didn't get a rabbit.

A few moments later, Sandblaster was in another dirty corner of Terraform 43 with G'Kay. They were alone, and Sandblaster wondered whether this dirty Svakken could be trusted. After all, his species weren't known for their polite manner and firm state of morals. He had no worries though, as he had a handy stun gun ready and waiting in his left...

"You should know I've already taken your stun-gun." G'Kay announced, holding aloft Sandblaster's pistol.

"I see..."

As G'Kay placed the passive weapon on a nearby waste unit, he began telling Sandblaster of the treasure he was seeking. It was in a far off corner of the Quadrants, although no one really knew where. All they knew were two things:

1 - that it was a very rare treasure indeed and

2 - that it was incredibly dangerous to find.

But Sandblaster liked danger. He liked it like a good rest and a packet of crisps.

"If there's danger to be had, stick it between two slices of bread and serve it up."

"What is 'bread'?" G'Kay asked.

"Oh. It's an Earth thing. Very nice. You'd probably like it."

G'Kay just grunted, and pulled out a document from own of his long, open sleeves. He passed it to Sandblaster who studied it over. It was a map, filled with co-ordinates and specific instructions that would take him to the

Asparia Galaxy, a light and hedonistic place filled with only the finest life forms.

"So this map, it'll take me to the treasure?"

"No." Snarled G'Kay. "It will take you to the person who *has* the map, to the treasure."

"I see... bit convoluted isn't it?"

G'Kay just shrugged his bony shoulders. "I suppose that's treasure hunting for you."

Sandblaster nodded. It certainly did add a fun spin on things, and he'd always wanted to visit the Asparia Galaxy again. It had been a while since... The Incident.

But that was the past, and now was the present, with treasure to be had in the future. Sandblaster thanked G'Kay, and gave him a big bag "full of riches". As he jogged off, collecting his pistol in the process, he pretended to ignore the Svakken as he ranted about receiving shiny trinkets instead of Tetras.

Sandblaster didn't have any to spare though. He needed the cash to find a co-pilot...

Frexia had its fair share of renegades who could help Kirk Sandblaster pilot a ship to the Outer Quadrants and beyond; despite the fact there was nothing actually beyond the Outer Quadrants. It was why they were called the Outer Quadrants. They were pretty much as far as space could go without going completely insane.

Or so Mad Bellax of Collia once said. But then all Collians were slightly mad.

There was no doubt that Sandblaster could buy one for cheap to boot. The wretched hive that existed within Frexia's many Terraforms all lusted after the sweet embrace of a handful of Tetras, and right now he had more than that. The question was, were they competent? Trustworthy? The kind of being you could count on when the chips were down and your chews were salted to within an inch of their taste?

Of course not. Which is precisely why Sandblaster jumped in his trusty ship, The Bounty, and blasted as far away from Frexia and its band of terribly terrible beings as quick as the thrusters would take him. Hire one of those bandits? You'd have to be a Collian.

Whizzing through the majesty of space, Sandblaster knew exactly where he was going. Back in his GAF days, swigging Cartereli's with the lads before slinking off and letting them pay the bill, they often spoke of the home of the "Lost Pilots". It was a place where maverick Flightsmiths went to perish on the wave of their own legacy. Burnt out, stretched thin and hung out to dry, they were any willing captains, for a price. And the price wasn't cheap. After all, these outcasts had all come for a reason, and were usually willing to stay.

That place? The floating bastion of jaded hope and lost souls.

Space Station Hull.

Named after a place back on Sandblaster's home planet where the anxious fear to tread, Space Station Hull was essentially a drifting condominium. It had it all for the lazy ex-aviator; cheap rooms, an open bar and all the TV stations in the known galaxy. Outsiders would come into its exclusive atmosphere and immediately turn back at the sight of a million accusing eyes. But should a man be brave enough and stick around, he'd become "one of the boys".

Sandblaster knew that if he'd find not only a pilot, but the best dang pilot there was, it'll be in Hull. After all, his old fighting buddy, Ziggy

Rodriguez, found his co-pilot there. A rather alluring Elejian called... well the name get's lost in translation.

"But Kirk," he told Sandblaster over several mind-spirits, "she can handle a ship like a..."

And at that stage Ziggy would burst into a low, guttural laugh and spasms in his elbows and eyes, which Sandblaster never quite understood. He assumed it had something to do with Ziggy and the Elejian's demise, when their ship crashed into an errant moon. The black box, when recorded, listed the cause of death as "Distraction".

Right now though Sandblaster was enjoying the ride. He wasn't a big fan of performing his own flights, but The Bounty's autopilot was good enough to let him cruise along and take in the scenery. And when it came to space, the scenery was like a first class meal in the restaurant of your dreams, where all your favourite dishes were on specials. It may have been the ales talking in his head, but Sandblaster sat back and took in the beautiful constellations and starbursts that erupted just outside his cockpit window. He saw as meteors flashed in the far distance, light years away but burning bright enough to look like they were right outside. He marvelled at the stars that shone in the great beyond, like landing lights to a world you hadn't yet made your name. Space had opened up many people's lives, and for Sandblaster it gave him a wealth of opportunity to appreciate the wonder of it all.

"BORING!" The Ghurians roared across the intercom.

While Xlaar tinkered away on some minor repairs caused by the pirates roving lasers and missiles, Sandblaster took offence to this interruption.

"I'll have you know it was very beautiful!"

"We don'ts want beauty! We wants treasure!"

Sandblaster shook his head with a smile. He envied these simple pirates, with their lack of appreciation for the finer things. Maybe one day he could educate them rather than have to blow them out of space before they did it to him.

"Sometimes, the *real* treasure is what you see outside your window..."

While Sandblaster wistfully stood there, everyone else went silent. After a moment, Xlaar turned to his comrade and laid one of his many hands on him.

"Kirk, that was the cheesiest thing I ever heard."

"Was glatting crud was!" The Ghurians spluttered.

"I have to concur sir that that was the single most schmaltzy-waltzy thing I have ever had recorded in my sound banks." Navi added, and he had recorded a lot.

Sandblaster considered their words, and then went back to the command.

"Navi, continue talking about how I was astonished by the beauty of those stars."

"Well that's the darn-tooting thing sir..."

For the stars that Sandblaster thought were landing lights, were landing lights. And right now his autopilot was careering right into the docking bay of Space Station Hull. Some intrepid documentarians would remember the time as "the day the innocence died", but thankfully Sandblaster managed to become aware of the situation and right The Bounty before any serious damage was made.

While several emergency sirens wailed behind him, Sandblaster sauntered into Hull with the swagger of a man who was ready to pay top Tetra for an experienced crewman. At least that's how it looked. Internally he was a bit wary of these folk, with their rough ways and tough talk. But, he knew that to at least get them on his side he needed to be confident. Surely then they would accept him as a fellow space adventurer.

He entered a bar adorned with several symbols denoting a language he wasn't immediately familiar with. This was of no matter to a man like Kirk Sandblaster though, who burst through the door and stood with his fists firmly on his hips.

"I'm looking for the best darn co-pilot you people have to offer!"

Every race stopped what they were doing and pointed their multiple, in some cases literally, eyes at him. All were suspicious, and none were welcoming.

Sandblaster surveyed them with a sly nod and changed tact.

"OK, the best darn PILOT you have to offer!"

Still, he was met by a wall of silence adorned with looks of menace. There were some nasty-looking characters in here; primarily a Ghurian with one look of disdain and another that said "I'll eat your ears." There was also a Zaarian, known for their ferocity in battle, whose second head was not favourable of Sandblaster at all.

But the treasure hunter was not to be put off so easily. He strutted to the bar, making sure to make firm, manly eye contact with every alien and fellow human who glared at him, and took a seat.

"Barman, I'll have a Catereli..." he said with a cocky grin.

"NVOJSN IUNJI VWFHNW WD O O O O!" Said the server, who was of Shorgan descent. A slathering race who had no concept of the idea of a lower jaw. Or, indeed, of slime retention.

Sandblaster's confident demeanour fell apart immediately, as it struck him what he had walked into. As the penny dropped he slowly turned to the shouting Shorgan.

"I think... your translator... is broken..." He whispered.

The Shorgan looked at him for a moment.

"NDSAT W WFOO QN AJ!"

Sandblaster smiled to those watching, but his frustration was building.

"I said. Your translator. Is bust."

"N IUJVQ!"

"TRANSLATOR! NOT! WORKEY!"

"How long exactly did this go on for Xlaar?" Sandblaster asked.

Xlaar sighed loudly. "Several hours..."

"Hmm, felt much shorter!"

Eventually the Shorgan got the gist of what Sandblaster was saying thanks to some creative use of glasses and interpretive dance. Sure enough, once the translator was re-adjusted to a more universal understanding, all the confusion went away.

"So what do you want?" The Shorgan bartender asked.

"A pilot! To serve alongside me on a quest for adventure."

The patrons grumbled at the sound of this.

"And also treasure!"

And with that, their grumbles abated. Suddenly Sandblaster was the most popular man in the bar, flashing his Tetras and sharing Cartereli's with many experienced plotters of space. But while he was enjoying the revelry, he couldn't help notice one person wasn't joining in.

The Zaarian seated at the far end of the joint.

"What's the matter big man, fun not your thing?"

One of the Zaarian's heads turned to Sandblaster while the other continued its stoic lament against the wall opposite.

"Come on... why not join in the application process?" Sandblaster said, gesturing to the drinkers around him who cheered in kind.

The Zaarian's other head turned this time, and all four of his eyes burned toward Sandblaster. He raised one of his four arms and pointed an accusing finger toward this human who had invaded his misery time.

"Because I don't want to engage in activities with an arrogant, cocksure, wannabe big shot human."

The atmosphere turned tense as the Shorgan hid behind his bar and Sandblaster's fellow merry-makers started to shift about uncomfortably. As for Sandblaster, he stood up, puffed out his chest and marched right up to the Zaarian. The alien made a dwarf of him, standing at least 2 feet higher in his bright red muscle-armour. But Kirk Sandblaster wasn't one to be afraid, and stood firm beside the Zaarian.

Then suddenly, with a slap of the Zaarian's hulking upper-left arm, Sandblaster beamed at him.

"I like you! You're hired! When can you start? How about now?"

The Zaarian stared at him in disbelief. Sandblaster just kept smiling.

"Why do you want me as a pilot when they've been buying you drinks all night?"

"Because you're the only one to resist my charms, and I respect that. You're not like one of those sozzled washouts who dance at the sight of a Tetra."

As soon as he said that, both Sandblaster and the Zaarian turned to the crowd at the other end. Their joyful partying spirit had turned sour at these words, and they were now hungry for a brawl.

"What's your name?"

"Xlaar."

"Kirk Sandblaster. Now," Sandblaster said as he rolled his sleeves up, "get ready to rumble..."

6

On the good ship Bounty, patiently followed by the Ghurian pirate ship that was being enthralled by Navi's tales, Kirk Sandblaster looked over at Xlaar with an expression that glowed with optimism. Xlaar had seen this look before, and knew it never ended well. In fact the statistical probability of it ending well had fallen so badly it was now in negative figures. Essentially, Sandblaster's "look of confidence" had defied the laws of numeracy and statistics.

It was that bad a look.

"Wait till they hear about our heroic fighting skills," Sandblaster whispered with a chuckle, "then they'll be absolutely terrified!"

"Xlaar sighed and dusted off his gloves. "You don't remember the fight do you?"

"I remember we left with our heads held high."

Xlaar smiled broadly across his two faces.

"There was a reason for that."

Carrying him out of the Shorgan bar by his armpits, his head high but lolling limply from his neck, Xlaar thought about stupid this adventurer really was and why he was now in his employment. Maybe it was the pride and loyalty that all Zaarians were bred with. The sense of honour that a Zaarian took not only into battle and other conflicts, but in food consumption and the noble art of love. In everything a Zaarian did, they did with the utmost integrity and upstanding behaviour. No matter the situation.

It was why when Xlaar double-head-butted his mouthy commander, he found himself at Space Station Hull, drinking the time away and taking the offer of a be-quiffed human with poor social skills.

Maybe that was why. A chance to redeem himself. With someone stupid.

The fight had started as any fight does, with a charge and shout of adrenaline that Xlaar had seen in many a clash. But he also knew that you make sure that you're never the one who's doing the charging and shouting and stuff. Sandblaster didn't know this, and Xlaar could only watch as the human ran full pelt into this motley group of various races and straight into the awaiting fist of a Rygan.

The noble Zaarian watched in awe as Sandblaster took the blow, staggered a few steps in a stunned trance, and then fell to the floor with a dopey smile on his face. After a few additional pummelling blows from the irate group, his ill-conceived allegiance to this knave took over and he let all four of his gloved fists clear house.

If any being will tell you anything, and they are wont to do so after a few, they will tell you never to fight a Zaarian. Not only do they have more limbs than the average race, save the spider-like Takaran's, they are almost always wearing their muscle-bound power-suits that they receive from birth. Designed to compensate for the weak, gecko-like bodies Zaarian's have, they are like combining as much brute force into one garment as galactically possible. They're so pumped, they make the Rygan's jealous. And you never make a Rygan jealous. Terribly sensitive they are.

After a few spinning clotheslines and thrown beings and smashed furnishings, Xlaar picked up the snoring Sandblaster and carried him out the bar before it got *really* out of hand. The Shorgan had slobbered something about a "tab", but a quick, harsh look from one of Xlaar's heads had settled that debt.

"I don't remember that." Sandblaster muttered, now feeling quite deflated and sorry for himself. As he made a comfort sandwich, Xlaar afforded himself a moment of superiority.

"I have some humdingers of additional information regarding that little rumble sir if you want to hear it!" Navi interjected.

Sandblaster didn't so much answer as grunt to himself, putting as much meat in his comfort sandwich as was humanly, or any other beingly, possible.

"It was from a report that was issued by Space Station Hull's security staff!"

Xlaar wanted to save Sandblaster's pride from any further punishment. But he was also still quite angry about this whole mess, so shut both his mouths and carried on listening to the now less-irritating voice of the ships computer.

"It describes the offenders, which would be your wunderbar self sir, as a 'hulking Zaarian warrior'..."

"I'll take that." Xlaar said.

"... and a 'wimpy, dumb as space vacuum human'! Would that be you sir?"

Sandblaster didn't answer, instead hearing the mocking laughter of the Ghurian space pirates out there in the dark heart of space. He took a bite of his comfort sandwich, only to have a barrage of meat smack him in the face when he squeezed the bread due to over-filling.

In his mind, Sandblaster thought about how this was not a fine day for Kirk Sandblaster.

"Now where the pickle-dee-dee was I? Oh yes! The Bounty..."

The Bounty awaited in Space Station Hull's port like an obedient dog waits for its master. However on this occasion, the master was completely unconscious and the dog was half-deaf, half-blind and half-insane. Nor did it take kindly to strangers.

As Xlaar entered with the blissfully asleep Sandblaster over his shoulder, he looked over all the ships that stood in the port. His breath was taken away and minds flooded with memories over some of the beautiful starship vessels that were there. Firebirds, Zippers, Stealthers and Blitzers, all stood proudly and strongly to take Xlaar and Sandblaster beyond the stars in style. Sure, there was the odd dreg or rust-bucket in between, but they were most likely there for repairs or scrap, dragged in by these shiny wonders for a few extra Tetras.

"Which one of these belongs to Sandblaster?" Xlaar bellowed at a nearby mechanic. Unfortunately he was a Drak, and thus cursed without the ability to speak. Mostly due to the fact Draks didn't have mouths.

Instead, the Drak just pointed, and Xlaar gasped as he beheld a purple-trimmed, ivory Firebird. It had everything Xlaar would need from a ship; two rear dual-sploders for full warp capabilities, destabiliser cannons when you need an edge in battle, and a glowing core that suggested more power than could ever truly be needed, and then some.

Xlaar adjusted the limp human on his shoulder and strode purposely to the ship, thinking about how maybe he had made the right decision in hooking up with this arrogant weirdo Sandblaster. Maybe his promise of treasure and adventure was a sure fire way to endear himself back on his home planet, and take back his rightful place as...

But before he could wallow more in his fantasies, the Drak came over and violently shook his head, doing his best to drag Xlaar's beefy arms away from the vessel. After Xlaar saw the weedy thing hanging there, he watched as it directed him to the ship next to the one of his dreams.

Once Xlaar saw it, he dropped Sandblaster and the Drak to the floor and swore very loudly in the Zaarian tongue. It was so shocking, even the nearby translators couldn't interpret it and instead it sounded more like:

"What an awful turn of events pilchard."

The Bounty was not the ship Xlaar wanted, nor any navigator with a sense of dignity would want. It was rustier than any piece of junk there, had the bare minimum needed to fly in Quadrant Space, and looked like if it saw combat it would explode out of fear rather than fight or fly.

Nevertheless, Xlaar was nothing but loyal, and picked Sandblaster up and entered the ship.

As he watched the hulking Zaarian and his human accessory enter, the Drak wanted to laugh. But as he didn't have a mouth, instead he thought of the amusement of it all and how he'd showcase it to his many wives later that eve.

Once on-board, Xlaar familiarised himself with the Bounty's controls. They were, as a Terraform agent might describe, "rustic", with a "retro" design that harked back to a "better, simpler era".

Xlaar was just scared if he pressed the wrong button the screen would pop off and his insides would be introduced to deep space.

His keen senses soon took over though, and Xlaar had the vessel in the air. Sure, it wasn't the best looking ship, it had many glaring health and safety violations for a start. But if he was to work with Sandblaster it would be *his* ship. A Zaarian was taught to find the pride in anything that was under his command, from the strongest warrior to the weakest. More often than not, Xlaar had been tested with commanding a bunch of oddballs and space-nerds in order to test his leadership skills. After several decades of hard graft and very few debilitating injuries, he would turn them into a fierce fighting force.

As he pounded away at buttons and thrust his mighty gloves over levers and power levels, Xlaar got back into the rhythm of being a pilot. He felt the buzz flow through his veins, as all four eyes glowed with passion. Seeing space rush past him outside made him feel complete again, part of a quest that would both challenge him and build his reputation. He would be like all Zaarian's before him, a legend that is passed down amongst the children to be exalted for millennia. He would stand tall with Erraa the Forthright, Kluur the Stern and Qiira the...

With a pathetic POP and slow, deflating hiss, the Bounty slowed down. All the stars that had blurred as Xlaar flew past suddenly came into full view, mocking him as he became stationary save for the soft lure of space itself.

He checked the controls, and double-checked them. There were no warning lights, no signs of trouble anywhere in the engines or otherwise. The warp core was still functional, the sploders still ready to splode. But the Bounty was no longer moving of it's own will.

With a start, Sandblaster finally came to with a shout of "Omelette!" Neither he nor Xlaar knew why he said "Omelette", seeing as he didn't even like eggs. But either way, the first thing Sandblaster noticed was the mild drift of the Bounty through space.

"What did you do?"

"I flew your wreck of a ship!" Xlaar firmly said, standing to attention. Sandblaster just looked at him confused, making Xlaar feel a little ridiculous.

Stupid tradition, he thought.

"If you were flying it, then why is it not flying?"

"It's your ship, you tell me! I mean I engaged the sploders, put all power to the core..."

In Sandblaster's concussed mind, the pieces all started to fall into place and he nodded and smiled at his new co-pilot.

"Well there's your problem my friend."

"What...?" Xlaar asked suspiciously.

"You tried to *fly* the Bounty, instead of easing it *into* flight."

Xlaar was stunned into silence.

"You see, you can't do your normal, cliché flying style in a fine ship like this. You need to feel it's different tweaks and quirks. Much like you would a fine ale or... whatever, you things partake in."

Xlaar was starting to see why the patrons of Hull would want to beat this guy up now.

"Ok... so what do we do now. Captain?"

Sandblaster took his seat at the helm and put his feet up onto the malfunctioning controls. Xlaar could only watch in horror as Sandblaster's boot knocked off a bit of holo-plastic revealing the warp cores true status: Terminal.

"Why don't we just sit back and see where gravity takes us. The true spirit of adventure!"

In that moment, Xlaar began to feel like he'd made a huge mistake, made more so when Sandblaster asked him if he wanted a sandwich...

"So long did you float for?" The Ghurian's asked, still so enthralled by the whole thing, that they had forgotten about the light issue of chasing Sandblaster for his wares.

"Who knows my nefarious chums!" Sandblaster answered with a dashing adjustment of his finely quiffed hair. "All I know is that it gave me and Xlaar some valuable time to get to know each other. I learnt of his rich, Zaarian heritage, one filled with the positive attributes you need in a loyal co-pilot. Integrity. Virtue. Other words that give you the feeling that this multi-limbed alien being is A-Ok."

Sandblaster rose from his chair and stood by his co-pilot's side while he tinkered away with various controls. It was all a vain attempt to trick the Ghurian's pursuit and get them off their tale, but both they and Sandblaster were enjoying Navi's tale too much to actually make it easy.

That, and the tethering technology they had latched on during the whole rambling saga.

"And what, dear Xlaar, did you learn about your new old pal Kirk Sandblaster?"

"That he's a dangerous fool who doesn't think." Xlaar said in dual-voice, without hesitation.

"Exactly!" Sandblaster said, oblivious to Xlaar's tone. "That I'm a renegade who shouldn't be messed with! I hope you pirates take that on board..."

"Just tell story!"

Drifting through the expanses of space had indeed given the two newly bound adventurers time to get to know each other. However while Sandblaster was casually impressed by Xlaar's record of combat, leadership and all-round skills, Xlaar was worried about his new cohort.

While in combat he had been fierce and eager to obtain victory, Sandblaster's story about aborting from his command ship before the Dark Quadrant made him nervous. As a Zaarian he wasn't used to such cowardice, but was also confused by the actions of the man.

Mainly because the Kirk Sandblaster who was humming a little tune to himself, while watching the stars slowly mosey past the crippled Bounty, didn't seem like a coward. He was too moronic to recognise peril, and in fact seemed to thrive on running *toward* it rather than away. The incident in Hull and his vocal love of "danger" all seemed to suggest a thrill-seeker rather than a wimp.

One of Xlaar's heads considered that this might be the reason why he hadn't jumped in the nearest escape pod. That this density of mind within Sandblaster, combined with his lust for adventure, excited the Zaarian. That there was a real possibility of danger around him, despite all the numbing frustration.

The other reason of course was that Xlaar didn't trust the escape pods. Like the rest of the ship, he had a feeling that once ejected he'd end up in the nearest sun. Or watched as parts of it went in different directions.

Luckily after a while of drifting in deep space, a freight ship passed them and Xlaar had managed to grab their attention. Sandblaster though was more suspicious, and obtuse about getting help.

"I'm sure after a while we'd end up where we needed to go. Let the waves of gravity guide us!"

"That might take years Sandblaster, and if I spent that long cooped up with you in here, I'd turn you into tiny, tiny chunks."

Sandblaster considered this for a moment.

"Hail the freighter!"

After a moments awkward tethering, as freighter crews were so thick they made Sandblaster look genius, the Bounty had gathered speed and was making its way towards the industrial planet of Nazia. Once a beautiful planet full of wildlife and luscious, exotic fauna, the kings of industry had recognised its potential for outsourcing and turned it into a smog-filled, grey mass.

Not that anybody really cared too much, as the whole Quadrant where Nazia existed was full of lush, breathable planets. The only exception to Nazia was a lack of giant, wild alien beings that tended to gobble up any visitors.

Like the industry heads had said: perfect for construction.

There, Sandblaster explained to Xlaar, they'd find the one man who could turn the Bounty into a floating, thrown-together pile of rust, metal and fusion, into something much, much more.

"A floating pile of rust, metal and fusion that WORKED!"

Xlaar shook his head with despair.

Once the duo arrived in one of Nazia's many spaceports, Sandblaster paid off the freighter crew with some of the shiny gems he still had left over. Luckily, they were just dumb enough to think them as expensive items. Or so

Sandblaster and Xlaar thought. You see, little did they, or any of the traders on Frexia know, but the gems were indeed highly valuable to the Gorts who ran the freighter. With his payment, Sandblaster had just made them millionaires for life.

But right now any life-changing financial transactions were far from the adventurer's minds. Sandblaster was eager to find the one man in this immense dimension that knew the Bounty nearly as well as Sandblaster did. It was the man who Sandblaster had bought it off, and indeed had kept coming to, despite his protests, ever since to fix it up every so often.

"That man is Obadiah Beansmith!" Sandblaster announced, to no one in particular but Xlaar assumed it was meant for him. "And he will gladly help us in our quest for glory!"

When Sandblaster found Beansmith, he was not glad to help him in his quest for glory.

"Why can't you just leave me be for, I don't know, forever?" Beansmith cried.

Sandblaster laughed a booming guffaw and turned to an intrigued Xlaar. "He always does this. It's kind of our thing."

Xlaar looked over the despondent human, who appeared to be ready to burst into tears at the sight of the cocksure Sandblaster. He was a shorter than average human male, dressed in dirty overalls and detachable cybernetic enhancements that helped with the whole mechanic thing. His face was covered in grime that etched out every layer of anxiety, stress and overall woe with the world around him. But despite that and a ruffled hairstyle that said "put-upon" rather than stylish, there was a look of hope in the man's eyes. It was as if all this toil would eventually spell some sort of happy nirvana on one of Nazia's other, more welcoming, planets.

Well, welcoming apart from the native Nazian's and their consuming ways.

Still, Sandblaster greeted Beansmith like an old friend, and indeed they were. Sandblaster told Xlaar how Beansmith had been the first mechanic he had encountered after he adopted his role of "Space Adventurer", and a combination of loyalty and cheap prices had kept him coming back. Beansmith though, looked more cautious about his "old friends" return. And so he should.

Over the years Sandblaster had, indeed, kept Beansmith in business, at the cost of his own mental health. Beansmith loved machines, it was why he was a space mechanic and why he spent so much time around them tinkering and tailoring to make them their very best. It was an emotional bond, and no bond was stronger than his with the Bounty. It had been his very first ship, a pet project he had begun in his formative years and continued to the very end.

Then Sandblaster had come along and seen the Bounty and declared it "the very ship for him!" Beansmith was reluctant to let go something that was so dear to him, but once Sandblaster had revealed the many Tetras he intended to pay, Beansmith's mind was swayed.

He justified the sale as a natural progression for the Bounty. The ship was meant to fly, and standing in his port as a beautiful piece of mechanized art was an affront to its core being. So Beansmith took the sizeable pay cheque, made Bounty the best it would ever be, and sold it to Sandblaster. And while the payoff was enough to put Beansmith up for life, he willingly agreed to make any repairs at a low cost for the swaggering adventurer.

But then came the first repair. Then the second, and third, fourth, fifth and so on and so forth, until the end of time.

Sandblaster didn't so much "look after" the Bounty; he used it as an industrial wrecking ball. Beansmith theorised once that even in the emptiest corner of space and time, Sandblaster could bash the Bounty into something.

And so a labour of love had turned into a beast of burden for Beansmith, and every arrival of Sandblaster to his port spelt another moment of care and attention to the child he gave away.

It was his cross to bear, and one that had broken him.

But Sandblaster still paid, and still held Beansmith as a close, and personal, friend.

"Before you get to the old bird, let's get some ales down your gullet Beansmith!"

"I... I don't want to drink. Not after last time."

Sandblaster blew him off. "So you ended up entangled with a cyborg lady-type, it's happened to us all!"

"She nearly killed me!"

"That's why you hook up with a cyborg! It's thrilling!"

"Oh no..." Beansmith sighed.

Xlaar decided to step in to save this poor human, grabbing Sandblaster aside.

"While he fixes the ship, we need to plan."

Sandblaster was confused, but then it hit him again. While they were on the hunt for treasure, they still didn't have a map. All they had was the map to the map, and the map to the map wouldn't get them anywhere except to the map that would lead them to the treasure that the map to the map promised.

There was a lot of mapping involved.

Luckily there wasn't much travelling.

"So where does this map lead to?"

Sandblaster looked at it, analysed it, and looked some more. He stroked his chin, nodded thoughtfully a number of times, and pointed his finger in a way that said "I'm thinking here, and I believe I have the answer."

After a long time of this, Xlaar took the map and saw where they had to go.

Nazia. The planet they were on. Just a short trans-warp away.

"Why was it taking you so long to look at the map?" Xlaar asked.

Sandblaster just looked off into the middle distance, earning the sudden unease of Beansmith standing by. He thrust his fists onto his hips and jutted his chin out with purpose as he bellowed into the stratosphere...

"I like, to look, at maps!"

And with that, Beansmith sadly shook his head and continued to re-fix the Bounty while Xlaar found the nearest trans-warper.

After a good old-fashioned once-over with the map, Sandblaster and Xlaar found the place they were looking for was on the other side of the planet Nazia. Luckily, inter-planet travel had improved since the creation of trans-warping, despite the difficult early stages of development.

It all started when the governing body of Universia was inspired by early Earth science fiction. Seeing shows that presented quick and easy travel via teleportation, the tech-savvy Martians were hired to create a similar sort of device. However, due to the expanding culture that the Universe was granting, Universia found cheaper labour in the far-flung planet of Diana. It's natives, a Neanderthal-like race of hairless humanoids, would work for forgotten promises rather than actual cash, thus making sure they secured the contract to build the trans-warpers.

However, while the Xdians were industrious, they were as intelligent as a pile of moon rocks.

Therefore, when the first test of trans-warpers was presented to the council of Universia, they watched with horror as numbers of Xdians stepped into the prototype, divided their cells across to another trans-warper in tiny, messy bits, and another would look confused and try the same thing.

Eventually, after a nasty hour of near constant nightmarish visions, the Martians were contacted to continue their work and sort the whole mess out. For a costly fee, of course.

Since then the art of trans-warpers have still been mired in controversy and casual wariness. In fact, many Psychopaths have accepted Transwarpaphobia as a serious, recognisable condition. At this juncture it should be noted that Psychopaths are not, in fact, the mad axe-murdering type that history defined them as, but a portmanteau of psychologists and telepaths, who exceed in the field.

Sandblaster and Xlaar gave each other a befuddled look. On the Ghurian ship, the dual-faced pirates gave themselves an equally confused one, which given their multi-faced status was very confusing indeed.

"Navi, why did you feel the need to clarify that?" Sandblaster asked.

"Well sir, just in case some non-future type person was listening in!"

"What do you mean, 'non-future type'?"

"I mean someone who is not from this exciting, science fictional world!"

"This isn't science fiction though you dumb piece of technology." Xlaar growled.

"Maybe so, but someone could be reading this and won't know of all these ram-dam-diddly future terms!"

Sandblaster and Xlaar stood there in silence for a moment, before looking over to the Fourth Wall. It was so called due to the fact it had the number "4" on it. After a moment considering the wall, which was always a really good place to sort ones head, or in Zaarians cases, heads, out, the crew returned to the story.

A quick consultation of the map to the map showed Sandblaster and Xlaar that they could find it in Nazia's 18th District. There was only one problem with this district: it had been turned into a giant dustbowl due to the expansion of industry across the planet. Ideally, it was agreed to be the "one green location" due to a contractual agreement by all the companies who had made Nazia Prime their home. However, what once was flush with green fields, glistening pools of water and cute wildlife which would frolic gamely across the vista, had been battered left, right and centre by the by-products of the surrounding factories and giant mechanical towers. The fields had turned grey with rot, the pools dried up and the cute wildlife was now either dead of mutated.

What was worse though, was that its tourism trade had dived right off the ledge. Legends told that still to this day, if you looked hard enough, you could find a labelled snow-globe. But who collects those really?

After having their physical masses deconstructed and then hastily put together again, Sandblaster and Xlaar arrived in the 18th District. Sure enough, they were greeted by wailing sands and a desolate landscape that stretched as far as the eye could see. Beyond the port where they stood, there was nothing except miles and miles of emptiness, and the only clue the map told them was that it was somewhere here.

Sandblaster tried looking confident, but his eyes betrayed him. They bugged out and shone with fear over the monumental task that lay ahead of them. Xlaar, on the other hand, was groaning and cursing loud enough to turn the air blue. Literally, as Nazia has an anti-profanity gas within the atmosphere. Here, one errant curse could earn you a large fine. At this moment though, Xlaar would pay that fine with a few handfuls of pain.

"Worry not my fine companion, as I'm sure they'll be some clue as to where the map is!"

"Where? IN THE SANDS?!?!"

Sandblaster swallowed hard. "Maybe..."

There was no looking past it, the two beings would have to suck it up and start combing the vast desert before them in the hunt for the map to the treasure. In his mind Sandblaster knew that this whole adventuring lark wasn't mean to be easy, but digging through miles of brown dust wasn't his idea of "fun".

Before the two of them set off though, an old Svakken emerged from a nearby port-house. His whiskers were grey and crumbling at the hint of a mild wind, and he wore a robe that almost encapsulated him. He called after the two adventurers, who were almost glad of the distraction.

"What are you doing?" He asked with a voice as worn as his clothes.

"Treasure old... man?" The Svakken nodded, and Sandblaster continued pleased at his efforts. He held up the map to the map and waved it about to get the Svakken attention. "This tells us that somewhere in this disaster zone lies a *further* map, to treasure."

"Oh." The Svakken muttered before reaching into his robe and producing a map. "You mean this one?"

To say both Sandblaster and Xlaar were dumbfounded would be an understatement. Sure enough, once unfurled by the old Svakken, the map was shown to be one pointing to the actual treasure. Star charts and all.

"Um. Yes. Yes that's the one."

"Oh, well here you go."

Sandblaster turned to Xlaar and looked quite pleased with himself.

"That'll be 1 million Tetras please."

At the sound of that lofty figure, Sandblaster slowly turned back to the old Svakken with a raised brow. Behind him, Xlaar visibly slumped, thinking of how he would lurch back to his home planet and how many years he could put up with the mockery.

"Don't worry Xlaar," Sandblaster said, the confidence returning to his voice, "I'll deal with this old leech."

"I'm a Svakken."

"It's a phrase!"

Xlaar wasn't sure what Sandblaster was going to do, but he didn't want to be around to find out. Beating up bars full of fellow pilots was one thing, but he drew the line at the elderly. He made his way to a nearby shack and collected his thoughts. Here he was, at a dusty waste on a polluted planet looking for a scrap of paper via another scrap of paper. If this was what adventuring was, he had been sorely mis-informed.

No sooner had he made himself comfortable, than Sandblaster appeared with a spring in his step.

"Well?"

Without uttering a word, Sandblaster flashed the actual treasure map and waited for the adulation from Xlaar. It didn't come, instead the Zaarian wondering what horrors this human had inflicted on the poor old Svakken.

No matter though, as they had their map and were well on their way to treasure.

All they needed was a working ship.

As it happened, Beansmith had performed a bang up job on the Bounty. The sploders were realigned and fitted with additional thermal charges for extra speed, the core was de-jigged and filled with enough warp power to blow them across the whole of space and back again, and best of all it had a new paint job. A sparkly crystal white. This bit made Xlaar especially happy.

As Xlaar took in the sight of his new command, Sandblaster and Beansmith were negotiating the little details via a small device in Beansmith's hand.

"Now I've fitted you with an AI windshield, for adverse conditions and the like."

"I like!"

"And your substance replicators now cater over an expanded number of cultural culinaries."

"Bon appetit..."

"Um, yes... well... the only other thing is the on-board computer."

"We don't need one with me at the helm." Xlaar piped up, feeling his self-belief puff up inside his power-suit.

"Yes, well, you say that but..."

Xlaar turned to threaten the small human, but Sandblaster intervened with a boisterous laugh.

"Enough you wacky dongbusters! Is the computer extra?"

"Um, yes?"

"We'll have it anyway. Better to be safe than in a million pieces eh Xlaar?"

Xlaar didn't respond. He was still in awe of the new, improved Bounty.

"Excellent, excellent... how do you want it?"

"Want what?"

"The computer?"

"I don't care."

"Very well..." Beansmith said, making sure to set the computer, known as Navi, to "extra annoying" in payback for all the years of abuse Sandblaster had put his ship through. "So now it's just the matter of payment?"

"Of course! Here's your fee." Sandblaster said, producing his Tetra-tablet to switch over funds to Beansmith. "Five hundred thousand Tetras!"

One of Xlaar's heads spluttered with surprise at the sound of this. He watched as Sandblaster finished the deal with Beansmith and let the nervous mechanic go back to his humble ways. As he made his way toward the Bounty, Xlaar made sure to stop him.

"I thought you said he was cheap!"

"He is! I've price checked..."

"But... that's a lot of Tetra!"

Sandblaster just looked at Xlaar.

"Wait... did you pay the Svakken as well?"

"What?"
"I thought you killed him!"

Suddenly the whole ruse had fallen apart. Sandblaster took a deep breath, and nodded. All Xlaar could do was use two of his hands to make sure his jaws didn't hit the floor too hard.

"I can't keep it secret no longer Xlaar, I'm rich."

"Rich?"

"As in very wealthy."

"How?"

"Don't you worry about that, we've got treasure to find!"

As Sandblaster boarded the Bounty, Xlaar just stood there stunned.

"If you're rich why are we going after treasure for?"

Sandblaster's head poked out the door with a smile.

"Adventure Xlaar! Adventure!"

"And that's the ring-a-ding tale of how I came to be on this fine vessel!" Navi announced, to disinterested silence.

Everyone, including the crew of the Ghurian ship, stood in silence, waiting for Navi to continue. But after a few, rather awkward moments, the Bounty's computer had stayed silent.

"Is end?" The Ghurians asked over the intercom.

Sandblaster and Xlaar didn't want to say anything for certain, but they had a feeling it was. Quietly, they nodded to each other and Sandblaster moved toward the intercom and went to speak.

"I think..."

"And now the thrill-a-minute bit when they went looking for the treasure!"

"Ooh I like this bit." Sandblaster cooed as Xlaar lost his temper again and slammed his fists against the Bounty's walls. While the adventurous Sandblaster made himself comfortable again, the Zaarian went to the rear of the ship. He was tired of all this now, and thought this was a good a time as any to catch some rest.

"So where the rock of Gibraltar was I?"

"Treasure!" The Ghurians called out, as engaged as Sandblaster was.

"Oh yes! So our wonderful adventurers finally had their map..."

And what a map it was. Your basic treasure map, which harks back to the bad old days of buccaneering, is a hastily scrawled affair with a few lines pointing to some crudely drawn doodles. This one though had it all; co-ordinates, star-charts, even the names and places of where they needed to go. As far as maps went, this was a premium effort.

Which made it all the more outlandish that Sandblaster, despite his already sizeable savings, decided to gamble it in a game of Light Run.

As Xlaar roared up the engines of the Bounty, ready to get into the heat of the pursuit, Sandblaster nursed his head where the hulking Zaarian had bashed him out of frustration. If Sandblaster had learnt one thing from this whole mess, it was that Xlaar packed quite the punch.

"Put on the ships computer, we'll get a lock on them!" Xlaar shouted.

"Xlaar, I think you'll find *I'm* the captain of this..."

Xlaar made a noise that sounded like a snort of derision, but implied to Sandblaster that if he spoke again he'd get another bop. Kirk Sandblaster did *not* want another bop.

"And I think that's a top idea! Navi, time to shine!"

Sandblaster punched a button on the Bounty's console and went to give Navi, the on-board AI that Beansmith had installed, his instructions. Instead he was met with the most chipper voice he'd ever heard across the galaxy.

"Well toodle-oo and hi-de-hi! My name is Navi and I am here to whittle your problems away!"

Both beings stared at the computer with horror, before adjusting to this annoying things tone.

"Navi, we need to catch that Firebird vessel that's zooming out of sight!"

"No problem!" Navi gleefully said, starting a series of beeps and bloops to signal his computing skills.

While he did so, Xlaar fired up the sploders and was launching the ship, when he made a simple, off-hand comment.

"How did we get in this mess...?"

"Well..." Navi began saying...

Back in the shiny days of the year 2012, Earth had regained its spirit of adventure. In the very, very past, it had looked to the skies...

"Navi, we don't need the history of the world right now." Sandblaster chuckled, shaking his head at Xlaar to try and instigate the humour of it all. "Let's just keep to recent history."

"Okey dokey sir! Well that all began when you wanted something to shovel down your flesh-hole!"

After leaving Nazia with their treasure map, Xlaar had taken to the fresh, new controls of the Bounty with ease. What he hadn't yet adapted to was the discovery that Sandblaster wasn't the hobo-like fool he had assumed he was. He was a Tetrillionaire with more money than sense. As Sandblaster explained once again, he wasn't in the adventuring game for the money; he was in it for the danger.

The explanation to his riches was simple. While travelling across space, Sandblaster had stumbled across many Tetra Bank Ships that had been raided by space pirates like the Ghurians and Rygans who were too stupid to crack open their vaults. Sandblaster though had a knack for such things, acquiring a great deal of free Tetras that he soon discovered had been written off anyway.

"One floating Tetra Bank became two, then three and four. I tell you Xlaar, the odds favoured me that day!"

"OK, so you're as dumb in luck as you are in mind, but that doesn't explain the thrill-seeking."

"What do you mean?"

"You deserted the GAF."

"Oh that... well I was bored."

"Bored?"

"Yes. Serving the GAF is such a drag sometimes. So I decided to jump!"

"So you're not scared of the Dark Quadrant?"

Sandblaster just laughed at this notion, and told Xlaar to pull the ship over. He had noticed a sign informing passing ships of a nearby Grub Lord, the fast food choice of every space adventurer. Not only did they have low prices, but they also had special flavourings that appealed to every race and being. Sure, the food was a grey sludge, but it was so darn tasty.

While Xlaar was hesitant to delay any further, he was also taken in by the garish neon signs and the promise of a sly bite. Besides, if Sandblaster was as rich as he seemed, they didn't need to get to the treasure any time soon. In fact, Xlaar was starting to come round to Sandblaster's laid-back style.

Grub Lord had become the core franchise across the galaxy, beating out such upstarts as Wally's and Ctolian Fireblasted Meats. The only true competition it ever had was the Earth based goliath known as O'Malley's, which was known for its aggressive business practises and callous nature when it came to providing healthy foods. In fact, when a customer would ask for the slimming alternative, they would find themselves blasted into the deep recesses of space.

It made for a lot of legal trouble.

However, Grub Lord found a clever way of taking over O'Malley's position at the top of the fast food chain. Its owner hired a fleet of Horgorians to the O'Malley's Space Station Headquarters, and paid them to blow the whole thing sky high. Indeed, if you go to that specific area of space today, you will see the one remaining O'Malley's sign that the Grub Lord owners left there as a sign of respect. Or perhaps a warning. Nobody's quite sure which.

Once inside, Sandblaster and Xlaar ordered their food and tucked in. Sure, visually it wasn't a pleasing eat, but the tastes invigorated them for the quest ahead. Not only that, but this Grub Lord served Cartereli Ale, and soon enough both Sandblaster and Xlaar were drinking merrily along with each other. They sang old Zaarian songs, which Sandblaster didn't understand, and told old, bawdy human jokes, which Xlaar didn't get.

Eventually though, a table of equally merry Brellians; a humanoid species from the Solaria Quadrant where Sandblaster hailed from, joined in. The group all revelled together, until one Brellian decided to up the stakes a little.

"Fancy a wager on some Light Run?" He asked, primarily at the more willing Sandblaster.

"Wager? I'll wipe the floor with you!" Sandblaster responded to cheers, and the game was on.

Light Run was a simple game, which saw players bet on what beams of light, spinning around in an infinite loop, would burn out first. The winner was the one who was still left shining, and Sandblaster had played it many a time back in his GAF days. He knew that the one you bet on was the one that was the dimmest at the start, for it would take more time to shine out. With that in mind, he made his choice and watched as the lights started spinning.

For the rookie Xlaar, it was mesmerising to watch the lights spin and shimmer in front of his eyes. The lights would glow softly at first, before beaming violently from within the Light Run game. Two lights went out one after each other, but both belonged to other Brellians. All that was left was Sandblaster and the Brellian who had suggested the bet.

"Let's raise it further!" The Brellian shouted, brandishing some sort of ticket. "You win, you get this code that opens any door you can find!"

"Excellent! And if you win, you get this map!" Sandblaster said, showing off the treasure map.

Xlaar was suddenly sobered up with concern. He nudged Sandblaster with two of his arms and moved toward his ear.

"Are you sure that's wise?"

Sandblaster just smiled. "Xlaar, I've never lost a game of..."

"You're out!" The Brellian cried, and sure enough Sandblaster turned to see his light had been extinguished. While he sat there despondent, the

Brellian grabbed the map and ran out with his friends, saluting his commiserations.

Xlaar was ready to explode, when he noticed something funny. A wire was extended from the game toward where the Brellian was sitting. Sandblaster noticed his gaze, and saw the wire for himself.

"He cheated! He blew the game!"

"WHAT?!?" This time Xlaar did explode, and grabbed a table and tore it from its foundations. After a brief freak out which involved a lot of questionable sounds, he grabbed Sandblaster and dragged him to the Bounty.

"Excellent story Navi!" Sandblaster said, quite enjoying his new computers way with words.

"Yeah, great, wonderful..." Xlaar sarcastically noted, doing his best to steer the Bounty through space and after the departing Brellians. "Now how about helping us catch them?"

"Sure thing partner!" Navi piped up. "They look to be going to the Haken Belt! Which is known..."

Xlaar slammed his fist down on the console and used one of his heads to look at Sandblaster sternly.

"Let's not ever turn that on again, OK?"

Sandblaster nodded in agreement. Although he decided to maybe float that rule should he ever need a bedtime story.

Either way, their destination was clear: The Haken Belt, and all the danger it provided.

While Xlaar navigated, Sandblaster started feeling quite excited about this whole scenario.

10

For your average space traveller, asteroid fields were not the ideal of flying locations. At best, they were filled with gritty irritants that clogged your sploders and other such points of entry. It was like sand on Earth, with little bits of debris finding its way into your pants, sandwiches, and even your lodgings weeks after the event.

At worst they were filled with colossal chunks of rock that, depending on the gravitational pull, would crush a vessel as flat as a very flat thing. Think of something very flat, virtually two-dimensional, and it would be even flatter than that.

The Haken Belt had quite the reputation amongst asteroid fields. It stretched across several planets in the Dilure Quadrant, dividing its rocky times between two separate solar systems. Several space cartographers tried to map it, but alas were met by the obstacles of time, money, and deadly space rocks that pinballed them around the dark, unforgiving space they inhabited. What they did find, from a safer distance, is that the Haken Belt was quite unique in the fields of asteroids. It was a Grade 5, meaning it was very dangerous indeed and filled with giant clusters of gargantuan rocks, but these rocks acted as tiny moons, or even planets. One such asteroid, christened Haken I, was found to have a small, moss-like life form within its craters. The green fluff would stay inactive on the rocks surface, not really moving but actually showing signs of intelligent life. It turned out that the reason it had evolved to such a state was not down to the harsh conditions of the asteroid itself, but pure laziness.

After this, they were mostly used in a consultancy role to the Universia government.

Nevertheless though, the Haken Belt was still a brutally dangerous place to navigate. The crushing debris moved with such a speed and force that only the most experienced pilot could weave through its unpredictable outlay, and live.

Thankfully, Sandblaster now had Xlaar on his side. As well as a *lot* of luck.

Back within the Bounty's cockpit, post-Haken Belt, Xlaar poked one of his heads through the door.

"That's a point, how are you so lucky?"

Sandblaster didn't quite understand the question, and resorted to using every ounce of his brainpower to try and work it out. After much space-staring and twiddling with non-existent beard hair, he finally turned back to his Zaarian chum.

"I'unno." He grunted with a shrug.

Xlaar was suspicious. He had seen a fair few things in this universe, but had never seen someone who came up rosy as much as Sandblaster. First the riches, then all the adventuring. Something didn't add up.

"Why do you ask?"

"Well, just when we were in the Haken Belt..."

"GAHGAHGAH!" Screamed the intercom, where the Ghurians were still listening in. "Spoiler! Spoiler!"

Xlaar muttered something and went back to his quarters.

They reached the Haken Belt to find no sign of the Brellians. Despite the lead Navi had given them, they had still trailed behind the Brellians, no-doubt stolen or hacked, ship. It wasn't the flashiest of models, but as Xlaar lamented it had probably been modded to within an inch of its natural existence.

Still, there they were, faced with an ever-evolving streak of dangerous asteroids, spinning and crashing against each other with the threat of destruction for whatever poor fool would decide to enter its arena.

"Full steam ahead!" Sandblaster announced, thrusting his foot onto his seat and pointing toward the cockpit window with purpose.

Xlaar chose to ignore him, rolling all four of his eyes.

Besides, there was no way the Brellians would have dared entered the Haken Belt. They weren't stupid. Indeed, they were devious fellows, with a penchant for dealing and double dealing. If they had led them to the Haken Belt, then surely a trap was afoot.

Xlaar tried telling Sandblaster this, but the human was more intent on trying out his latest toy.

"Shall we turn Navi back on? He'll know the score..."

"No." Xlaar stated in unison.

"Spoilsport."

Instead of using Navi, Xlaar preferred to trust his many guts. The Brellians were out there, waiting for them to make a mistake and then vanish into deep space with their map. He felt determination fill his veins, a thirst for vengeance making his mouths dry.

Sandblaster was more casual in his approach. He had taken to studying the Haken Belt, watching its giant rocks clash against each other, smashing apart and creating smaller, tinier rocks. Each time a collision would happen, a new series of asteroid debris would be formed. It was like the circle of life, if indeed crusty mass could be defined as life.

While Xlaar was fussing and fuming over the random nature of the Belt, Sandblaster was conjuring an idea. He noted that one asteroid was the size of a small planet, and home to many a Haken no doubt. If that was true, and he was pretty sure it was, then that would mean deep craters...

"Navi! Fire all weapons at that asteroid over there!" Sandblaster shouted, once again thrusting his digit strongly past the cockpit window.

Xlaar turned to face him as he stood there, half pointing and half posing. Probably more posing than anything. There was never a photographer when you needed one.

"Why are we shooting an asteroid and risking creating a catastrophic blast of asteroids?"

"Because of reasons."

"Which are?"

"Vengeful!"

"You do know that if Navi is turned off, he can't shoot. Right?"

Sandblaster didn't know this, and cursed the fact his on-board computer wasn't automated to his fine, dulcet tones. No matter, he'd tell Beansmith next time.

"Then Xlaar, fire up the blasters and shoot the mojo out of that mass!"

Xlaar wasn't sure, but he also respected the chain of command. Sitting at the attack controls, he punched in the location of the asteroid and started charging the blasters beams. While the blasters sounded excessively violent, due to the Universia Peace Code they were only designed to stun and demobilise. Thankfully though, when it came to this particular celestial construct, it would blast it to smithereens.

"What do we do if it throws more asteroids at us?" Xlaar asked before firing.

"We blast them too!"

Xlaar had a bad feeling about this. But, in spite of a moments pause, he fired the blasters.

Bright beams boomed out of the Bounty's blaster cannons and hit the giant asteroid square on. There was a moment's wait, before it exploded in a smoky mess of debris and moss-covered chunks. If the residing Hakens had the inclination to speak at this sudden turn of events, they'd most likely be asking "WHAT ON THE SEVEN MOONS OF CTOLIA IS GOING ON?!?!?"

Luckily, they were too lazy for this, and just enjoyed the ride.

Sure enough, smaller rocks threw themselves at the Bounty, which Xlaar did his best to deflect. While he was a good shot, he wasn't good enough to hit several fast-moving objects at once, and so when the Bounty's shields wailed at them there was no surprise.

"We're taking heavy damage Sandblaster! We need to leave!"

But Sandblaster wasn't listening, he was looking. And he had just seen what he was looking for.

"There!"

Right in front of them was the Brellian ship, thrown tumbling from the now destroyed asteroid. It had taken residence in one of its many craters, as Sandblaster had deduced, and was now struggling to retain some sort of control of itself.

Xlaar was impressed, and when Sandblaster told him to pursue in spite of the immense risks they had now created, he no longer hesitated. The thrusters were pushed to full, and the Bounty tore toward the Brellian ship. They were ready to tether to it, board, and reclaim the map they had worked so hard to get. Xlaar may even lay down a few friendly warnings using his might power-suit gloves as well.

"I gotta say Sandblaster, I'm impressed." Xlaar admitted as they flew to intercept the Brellians, who were now spiralling deep into the Haken Belt.

"What can I say good buddy, I have an eye for a good idea! Now, all we need to do is catch those Brellians and..."

Before Sandblaster could finish, both he and Xlaar watched as the Brellian ship they were fast heading toward was crushed between two rather large asteroids. As predicted, its voluminous form soon became much, much thinner, before imploding in a rather nasty, if not pretty, explosion.

As both beings looked on stunned, another couple of large rocks were starting to flank them.

"Um. Retreat?"

Sandblaster needn't have asked, as Xlaar had already reversed the sploders and was veering in and out of any obstructing asteroids. They had gone far too far into the Haken belt, and now every movement needed to be both cunning and fortuitous. Asteroids seemed to fling themselves at the Bounty, hitting it so hard the noise reverberated throughout the ship.

Xlaar steadied himself in his seat, desperately trying to bring the ship under control and avoid further damage. Sandblaster had been less forward thinking, and was now experiencing the thrill of being thrown around the cockpit like a rag-doll.

In his mind, he thought it rather fun. But then he did suffer quite heavy cranial damage.

A few smooth moves later, and the Bounty was clear of the Haken Belt, just before several asteroids collided and smashed anything in its path. Both of the crew took a breath, with Sandblaster doing his best to rejig his brain, but failing miserably.

"Bananas." He said, eyes crossed.

"That's all well and good, but what about the map?"

Sandblaster took a deep breath, asserted himself, and once again pointed into the deep recesses of space.

"We wait!" He declared, before passing out onto the floor.

"You wait a lot!" The Ghurians piped up.

Sandblaster couldn't help but agree, but then to him waiting was the very nature of adventuring. For him, no true adventure simply came instantly. Sure, you could be a thrill-seeker who threw himself into the nearest danger and did his best to risk his life. And that did sound rather good. Very good, in fact. Sandblaster made a mental note to do this next time the opportunity arose.

But yes, while Sandblaster thrived on danger and adventure, he didn't take stupid risks, despite his reputation. He wanted to explain to the Ghurians that he *could* have jumped in his spacesuit, dived out of the Bounty and defied the peril of finding a small map in the unforgiving tag team of space and giant asteroids. He *could* have done this, but for one problem.

He never bought a spacesuit. They were terribly unfashionable, and he didn't want to be caught on camera looking less than dashing.

"Don't you worry my plunderous pursuers..." Sandblaster said with a smile. "Things are about to get a lot more excitable!"

The Ghurians were unsure, but decided to carry on listening anyway. Sure, they could blast the Bounty, jump on board, and then beat up Sandblaster and Xlaar, but they had time to spare.

"Human did say it get excite." The Ghurian captain said.

Outside the devilish cataclysm known as the Haken Belt, where many a ship had met its crushing demise, including the recent Brellians, the Bounty stood firm. It watched, it waited and most of all, it made some sort of low level humming noise that you can't hear in space, but definitely happens. It's in the manual.

On board, there was a hive of activity as Xlaar was conjuring up plans to find the lost map. If indeed, there was still a map to find. The Brellian ship had been pretty effectively destroyed, and there was a pretty good chance a flimsy bit of paper would be torn apart by such an event.

But, as ever, Sandblaster was confident.

"It's paper, so it's already flat." He theorised, reading a space ship magazine that Beansmith had left behind. "Besides, it's also laminated."

Xlaar did his best to turn Sandblaster's words into white noise.

The Zaarian's plan was simple, if ultimately foolish. Using one of his laser pistols and his power-suits anti-vacuum attributes, he would propel himself out the ship and into the Haken Belt. There, he would blast asteroids away with gun and power-fist until he found this darn bit of paper that would lead to their treasure. It was insanity, and one of his brains knew this, but if he spent one more moment listening to Sandblaster try to sound like he knew what he was reading, all "turbo-sploders" and "Drift Ship Expo's", he'd be propelling him out. Without a suit.

Before he could launch into his plan though, Sandblaster finally realised what he was doing.

"Are you leaving?"

"Yes."

"Why?"

Xlaar did his best to bite his tongues and instead answer rationally. "We need to find that map."

"Ah it's only one map." Sandblaster responded, putting his feet up on the controls console.

Xlaar felt himself blister with rage, but did his best to keep control.

"We worked pretty hard to get that map."

Sandblaster scrunched his face up. "Not really."

"... Ok maybe not *pretty hard*, but there was effort! And a Zaarian never gives up!"

Sandblaster laughed a laugh than can only be described as "oh you silly thing". He put down his magazine and strutted up to his new comrade, a look of friendly sympathy on hand.

"That's the problem with you Zaarian's. Always so engaged in everything. It's always a quest! A mission that must be finished! Never failed! So uptight..."

"Keep talking little man..." Xlaar warned, all four fists clenching.

"Look, I mean no disrespect, but if you're part of my crew you gotta relax. Alleviate all this 'honour and pride' stuff that your people ingrain on yourselves. Learn to live a little!"

"You want me, to forget several life-times worth of tradition and teaching? Something passed, from generation, to generation?"

Sandblaster beamed a big, goofy smile. "Yes!"

If Xlaar was a more violent man, he would have punched Sandblaster straight through the Bounty's walls. Instead, he found the human's chummy demeanour to be, actually, warming.

Shockingly, Xlaar found himself beginning to smirk. Even titter. Before long, he was guffawing. It was a strange sound and one that, at first, absolutely terrified Sandblaster. Zaarian's rarely laughed, and when they did it was a queer, hooting noise that went from baritone to falsetto in seconds.

He let the big alien let it all out for a moment, before settling him down and thinking over a more reasonable plan than asteroid blasting suicide.

"We could always drive the ship in there and blast away." Xlaar offered as an alternative.

"Less blasting, more not blasting." Sandblaster replied, before wagging his finger with glee. "I could *pay* people to fly in there, distracting the asteroids!"

"That's both insane and truly frightening."

"You don't think they'd do it?"

"With the amount of Tetras you could offer? I'm worried about those that would."

Xlaar continued to point out the vague evilness within Sandblaster financially-motivated scheme, and the two continued plotting.

As they sat there, musing over ways to find a very small map in a very dangerous, and very large, area of space, something strange happened. The two beings bonded. Despite their differences, Sandblaster being a renegade, devil-may-care human and Xlaar being an uptight, regimented Zaarian, they found a common ground in their lust for adventure. Especially over the small issue of money.

Xlaar was intrigued though, if he was so rich then what did Sandblaster do with all the money?

"I give it to small, needy children, across the galaxy."

"Wow. Really?"

Sandblaster looked very serious before bursting into laughter. "No, I spend it!"

Xlaar shook his heads.

While they traded stories, with Sandblaster talking about his post-GAF days travelling the universe and Xlaar explaining his departure from his home planet and eventual arrival at Space Station Hull...

"Why aren't you telling those stories? They're very cool!" Sandblaster argued.

"Would you like me to fully explain all the various exploits and scrapes both you and Xlaar have gotten into over the years?"

Sandblaster considered this. "How long would it take?"

"By my estimations, 320 years!"

"Carry on with the original tale."

So, while Sandblaster and Xlaar found out they were not so different, in the vast vacuum of space and against all known logic, including the infallible logic of the all-knowing Hyustians, a pair of asteroids collided in the Haken Belt, shattering each other into tiny pieces and uncovering...

A piece of paper.

Not just any piece of paper of course, but a piece of paper that was soon disintegrated by flailing chunk of rock from which it was birthed. Luckily, neither Sandblaster nor Xlaar noticed its destruction. And even if they had, luckily it was just a betting slip that one of the Brellian's had in his pocket.

No. The piece of paper Xlaar noticed out of one of his eyes came after one of the pieces of debris was shattered again, uncovering the map.

After lots of screaming and shouting and multiple finger pointing and Sandblaster saying "what is it boy", the adventurer saw it for himself.

"Tiny rocks!"

"Past the tiny rocks!"
Sandblaster squinted and then shouted again. "The map!"

From there the plan was set. It was a simple plan that required much thinking, cunning and preparation.

Xlaar jumped out of the Bounty in his power-suit, armed with a pistol, and blasted away a few small asteroids to grab the map.

As Sandblaster watched him destroy chunk after chunk of space rock, he couldn't help but think that this original plan may not have been an all round bad one. At least that's what he would have thought, before he saw a colossal beast of an asteroid head toward Xlaar and quickly had to pull him back.

As the Zaarian crashed back into the relative safety of the Bounty, Sandblaster grabbed the map. He instantly wished he hadn't, as it was fairly frozen from being out in deep space. He swiftly dropped it to the floor and dunked his hands in some Thermal Aqua. While his hands steamed back to a normal temperature, both captain and co-pilot looked at the map.

The instructions were simple, and as it happened they were a short space-ride away from finding their treasure. After a quick rinse of the hands, Sandblaster keyed in the co-ordinates and sat back with a smile on his face.

"So where's our destination?" Xlaar asked.

Sandblaster didn't answer, instead theatrically using his finger to turn on Navi.

"Good day to you!"

"Navi, where are we heading?"

"Why I'm pleased as punch to inform you good fellows that this ship, according to these handsome numbers, is now heading towards... The Dark Quadrant!"

Xlaar watched with amusement as Sandblaster's eyes went wide and all the swagger in his smile snapped away. He even afforded himself another little laugh, which probably didn't help Sandblaster's nerves anymore...

And so, with both sploders firing into action, the Bounty made its way...

To the Dark Quadrant!

"I thought you didn't fear anything?" Xlaar asked, faintly amused at Sandblaster's nervous reaction to the news of heading to the Dark Quadrant.

"I don't."

"Then why are you scared of going there?"

"I'm not."

"Then why are you nervous?"

"Because... I need the loo."

With that, Sandblaster jumped up and went to the toilet. It was a fair few minutes, stretching to an hour, before Xlaar opened the door to find Sandblaster sitting there, sulking.

"What's the problem?"

Sandblaster took a deep breath and rose from the toilet, forgetting he did actually go and hadn't yet done up his trousers. After a quick pull and adjust of his clothes, he carried on his important speech.

"The Dark Quadrant represents a lot to me Xlaar. It represents failure. It represents the day my life changed. Most of all, it represents dark..."

Xlaar let this sink in before asking the obvious question. "Are you afraid of the dark?"

"What? No!" Sandblaster cried, suddenly feeling very defensive.

"Then what's wrong with the *Dark* Quadrant?"

It was actually the unknown that perturbed Sandblaster. Since his evacuation from the GAF on the outskirts of that unknown part of space, nobody had dared enter it. The stories went around about the lost fleets, the monsters that may lie within. And most of all, in Sandblaster's own words:

"They heard that if the fantastic Kirk Sandblaster won't go in, it must be bad news."

Xlaar, having found his sense of humour, let out another raucous laugh. Luckily for him and the ships general hygiene, Sandblaster was still in the toilet.

Travel to the Dark Quadrant was annoyingly swift for Sandblaster. He was quite happy with the relative excitement that the Dilure Quadrant provided and had no wish to trade that in for vaguely charted territory that had become the Bermuda Triangle of space.

Since Universia had begun their charting of known space, the Dark Quadrant had become the biggest obstacle. The edges were certain, allowing the likes of the Dilure, Werrat and Earth's home, the Globa Quadrant to all mark out where, exactly, the Dark Quadrant started. It was so called due to its starless space, a desolate void that consumed anything that went into it. There were some who said that the sudden change in atmosphere, from a celestial plateau to an empty darkness, drove some beings mad.

Mind you, that was from the terminally insane Collia. Although they did write the book on madness, called "So You're Nuts: Or How Actually Really Are".

There was a lot lost in translation from all the random scribbling.

Nevertheless, the Dark Quadrant had its edge, and few entered it. As the Bounty approached, Sandblaster's veins chilled at the sight of it. Pure, unrelenting black. The true absence of space, and by extension, life. He didn't like it, not one bit, and considered how quickly he could make it to the escape pod before Xlaar would drag him back.

But he wasn't scared. He was just wary.

Maybe it wasn't the fact that it was an unknown adventure, rather that it was the last adventure. The final frontier, as some would say. Apart from uncharted space, which he had found quite boring when he attempted to chart it, the Dark Quadrant was the last place where man or being had ceased to try and conquer in the big, wide universe.

Upon entering, he would risk being lost to the bleak landscape that so many had been lost to. A place without a sun, and thus without light.

Sandblaster didn't like it.

Xlaar, on the other hand, was made of sterner stuff. He saw the black landscape of the Dark Quadrant and suddenly felt a burst of pure pride. This was the adventure the human rogue had promised, and it was now more than mere treasure. It was about discovery, venturing into a place that no-one else had ever seen and lived. The thought of ceasing to exist in the act of such a perilous mission gave him a thrill. Should he be lost, he'll be seen as a hero, who gave his life in the spirit of pioneering.

This wasn't about action; this was about something much, much more. Something Xlaar had never had the pleasure of experiencing.

He *did* like it.

"You know," Sandblaster spoke up, his usual cocksure nature wavering a little in his voice, "I hear there's some really great treasure over in the Werrat Quadrant. Fun to get to boot, with battles and nasty beings and loads of..."

With a punch of the console, Xlaar pushed the Bounty into the black of the Dark. Sandblaster was thrown back with the force of speed and tumbled back into the Relaxation part of the ship, knocking over a few bit of loose furnishing.

As the stars vanished to be replaced with the endless void, Xlaar turned to the human. He suddenly saw how small and puny he was compared to his buff, Zaarian physique, and felt a little pity for him. For a moment, he considered the fact that he would have to look after this little man. To save him, possibly from himself.

Walking over, he held out one of his many hands for Sandblaster to get up. He took it, and stood side-by-side with the gecko-like warrior, nodding his appreciation.

"Xlaar, I just want to say, if anything bad happens, well..."

"SCREEN TINT UP TO 4000%" Something said.

"Huh?" Sandblaster murmured as he and Xlaar turned to face the cockpit window. Before they could respond, they were hit by a burst of light that sent Sandblaster to the floor again, clutching his eyes.

Sparks danced in the dark of his eyelids. The brightness that had struck him was so intense, so fierce that it had stunned him into blindness. Sandblaster clawed around, trying to get his bearings, but his mind was shouting words that he didn't understand. Every effort to open his eyes ended with several coloured blurs and another journey back to the Bounty's floor.

"Xlaar! What's going on?"

"Where are you?"

"I'm over here!"

"Where's 'here'?"

As Sandblaster slowly got up, holding his hands out for balance, he felt one of Xlaar's suit-bolstered arms smack him in the face. He was starting to become good friends with the floor.

"What was that?"

"My face!"

"Nothing important then!"

Sandblaster paused for a moment, covering his eyes with his arm for extra shade.

"Why are we shouting?"

Xlaar took a moment to respond. "I don't know."

It took a few more moments before both beings sight came back, if a little longer for Xlaar and his multiple eyes. As Sandblaster steadied himself against a chair, he looked out into the cockpit of the Bounty with squinted eyes.

Outside, was the brightest, most vibrant sun he had ever seen. Its size was incomparable, given that it's surface took up all that Sandblaster could see.

"Navi? What level is the cockpit's tint up to?"

"Why that would be a shadowy 4500%!"

Sandblaster was stunned, but managed to collect himself to turn it up a bit more.

At 5000% tint he finally managed to get a good look at the mega-sun that was before him. Sure enough, it was the largest surface he had ever seen, with no hint of an edge to it, no matter where he looked. What amazed him further was the fact that periodically, little black dots would pass by, small enough to be almost insignificant but noticeable all the same.

Sandblaster knew exactly what the dots were. They were planets.

When Xlaar joined him he was as in awe of the mega-sun as Sandblaster was. All the two beings could do was stand there and watch as the planets and moons around it passed by like flies against an Earth sky. Even with the high amount of tint, the sun still dazzled.

Xlaar quickly theorized what had happened to the previous ships. They hadn't had the benefit of one of Beansmith's tint additions. It was a needless thing to have, given the general dimness of space, but in this instance it had saved their lives. Taking stock of their surroundings, many derelicts floated aimlessly by, no longer manned and just ghosts of a previous time.

With a deep sense of pride, Xlaar knew that they were the first beings to see this beautiful part of space.

"Bet it gives a heck of a tan!" Sandblaster quipped with a nudge.

But actually he was very wrong. While the Dark Quadrant, which would now require renaming lest it forever be mocked, had a very, very, very large mega-sun, it was also a Cold Sun. Cold Suns were rare, in that they had reached a level of heat that had broken the laws of physics and instead turned it cool. They gave off the same amount of light, but were about as warm as an icicle in space.

Which was very cold indeed.

As the two beings took in the wonder, Sandblaster clapped his hands together.

"Right!" he announced, "Time to find some treasure..."

13

On the other end of the communications link up with their pursuers, the Ghurians were getting restless.

"Finally! Treasure! Where treasure?"

"Look, you can't just *have* treasure." Sandblaster went about explaining, "You must *earn* treasure, and sometimes that requires some back story."

"TREASURE!" The Ghurians roared back, their voices crackling due to the excessive volume.

"Are you not enjoying the tale?"

"... yes."

"And if I told you there were further twists?"

The Ghurians stayed silent, scolded like petulant children which to be honest, was the level of their intelligence.

"I thought so." Sandblaster smugly said to himself, leaning back in his chair.

Beyond the cockpit, in the Bounty's relaxing quarters, Xlaar was doing his best to rest through this whole saga. He wasn't one for long monologues and bedtime stories, and besides he had heard this one before. But then again, it was nice to hear about how Sandblaster had made him discover the joy in life, and made all the stress of the Ghurian battle melt away.

He may have even got some sleep, before Navi continued by shouting...

BANG!

Before Sandblaster and Xlaar could relax upon their entry to the bright lights of the Dark Quadrant, the Bounty was struck by something very heavy and very hard. As sirens wailed to alert them to some mild structural damage, par for the course these days, Sandblaster looked around in panic as Xlaar steadied the controls with all four hands.

"Talk to me!"

"Hello!" Navi said.

Xlaar replied with his fist, silencing the on-board computer once more. He turned to Sandblaster who was looking out the left hand side of the cockpit window.

Debris. More specifically a lost GAF fighter that was now limply part of the mega-suns orbit. It hadn't quite smashed into them, but the sheer bulky design of a GAF fighter had reacted badly with the delicate Bounty. Worse, it had knocked them off course, sending them in a zero gravity tail spin and right into trouble.

Trouble in the form of an ever-increasing ball of gas.

While normally gas is quite a welcome state, given its relative lack of form, in some places it was actually seen as quite a deadly force to physical objects. While yes, some Scientists would comment about the toxicity of such things, a spaceship would normally have nothing to fear given the inherent sustainability against outside forces. However, as some ships learnt while trying to make first contact with the planet Daetra, and its gassy outer atmosphere, some gases didn't mix well with ships. In the instance of Daetra, it had melted them all down to a rather odious goo that some culinary experts would argue could be "quite the taste sensation".

So, if you found yourself heading towards a large area of unknown gas in an unknown Quadrant and were already quite stressed given the fact that desolate spaceships designed for warfare were prone to crashing into you... well you'd be a bit concerned.

Sandblaster, doing his best to cling to anything cling-able while Xlaar battled the forces of space, pulled the map from his pocket and smiled.

"Perfect!" He shouted with a smile only he could smile. "We're on course for the treasure!"

Xlaar was utterly confused. "What are you going on about?"

Sandblaster pointed to the growing ball of gas they were seemingly being dragged to. "It's a planet! A gas planet no doubt! I'd muster that from all the gas it has..."

Xlaar gritted his teeth.

"According to the map the treasure is buried there, or as buried as you can be in gas!"

A Gas Planet was actually a regular occurrence in deep space. It happened when a small mass, maybe an asteroid or bit of debris, found itself covered in a gas which, as the object orbited, grew in size until it was large enough to qualify under Universia's planetary laws. The largest known one was, funnily enough, in the Globa Quadrant, and originally thought to be a "second Earth". Of course once ships tried to land and ended up crashing into each other due to the whole lack of physical planet, everyone had a jolly old laugh and created the idea of a Gas Planet.

To Sandblaster, the whole equation was falling into place. The treasure wasn't in the Gas Planet, it was the Gas Planet. Instead of a random chunk of rock or one of these GAF fighters, the hold had formed the nucleus and the gas had encompassed it.

"So you're saying," Xlaar said as he struggled to fight the excessive force the planet was producing, "that to get the treasure, we have to destroy a planet?"

"Effectively!"

Xlaar smiled. "I kinda like that."

Sandblaster gave him a wink. "So do I!"

The only issue now was trying not to plunge too fast into it to destroy the Bounty. Besides, the two adventurers still had no idea what type of gas they were being pulled into. Luckily, Xlaar's piloting skills yielded a plot.

Using his knowledge of basic physics and angles, Xlaar made one of the sploders blast heavier than the other, causing the Bounty to turn away from the Gas Planet. After that, they were now facing the GAF debris that had started this whole ordeal. Xlaar punched in the command, and the Bounty locked a gun toward the debris. The other aimed slightly to the right.

"Hold on!" The Zaarian roared, and fired.

Two missiles fired at once, and exploded in unison. The one to the right caused enough force to push the Bounty away from its current trajectory, and into another gravitational field. To aid this further, the other missile had missed the GAF wreckage, instead exploding just behind it. This caused it to be propelled forward with great speed, throwing it further into the Gas Planet's pull. It didn't buy much time, but it bought enough to watch whether they were about to become space soup or merely slightly stinky.

The two watched with baited breath as the GAF fighter dived into the denser part of the Gas Planet, while they were slowly being slingshotted back into it. As the force around it sparked flames around the ship, it was almost a relief to see it enter without a major issue. Which was lucky, as they were now about to go in head first themselves.

"Well, time to get gassy!" Sandblaster said, with far too much enthusiasm.

Xlaar did his best to slow their entry with the Bounty's sploders in full reverse mode, but still the cockpit window steamed with the burning of planetary arrival. Sandblaster just did what a good captain would normally do, watch to see what they'd encounter and most of all, have a cool beverage. Beverages, and sandwiches, were key to good captaining.

The Gas Planet was thick with fumes, typical of the state of matter. At times, it was tricky to see what was in front of Sandblaster's very eyes. The gas was mostly colourless, save for a few flashes of vivid greens and golden yellows, although Sandblaster thought that may be his eyes playing tricks on him. Some of the sights you see in deep space were so incomprehensible, your brain did it's best to fill the dots, and with a Gas Planet there were a lot of dots.

Sure enough, the smell radiated through the Bounty's walls. It wasn't unpleasant, but there was an off-putting aroma to it. Like good meat that had *just* gone off, or some body spray that was off brand. But this was no time to take in the fundamentals of the Gas Planet, although Sandblaster had considered naming it after himself. After all, Kirkia had a ring to it.

No, what mattered now was finding the treasure, and destroying Kirkia before it had a chance to live.

Taking the centre of a Gas Planet was no easy task, as you risked setting off a cataclysmic chain reaction that could either end in complete desolation of the universe, or if you were really lucky, a little black hole. If the treasure hold formed the centre of this Gas Planet, and Sandblaster was pretty sure it was, then they'd need some smooth moves to get it out and escape before finding themselves in a pretty dicey scenario.

"There!"

Sure enough, Sandblaster was right. In the deep heart of the Gas Planet, shimmering in its fumes as the gases circled violently around it like a nasty storm, was a hold. It was essentially a steel crate, but treasure holds were so securely fastened that it was of no surprise, that in its new life in deep space, it had become the core of a planet. They were just that tough.

The tricky task now was getting it.

Sandblaster explained the consequences to Xlaar, and both agreed that it would take all their cunning, all their skills and all their bravery to attempt such a heist. Sandblaster turned to Xlaar, and looked him in the eye with every bit of manliness he had.

"Most of all Xlaar, we could very well die. And if so, I want to say..."

"Is that the GAF ship?" Xlaar asked, his other head looking out the cockpit window.

The two watched as, indeed, the GAF ship they had snookered to test the gases toxicity had plunged right past the Gas Planet's treasure core, thrown itself out the other side and then been snapped back in. This time though, it was on a crash course with the hold.

In a bizarre turn of events, Sandblaster and Xlaar watched with shock as the GAF ship slammed into the hold, causing a brief moment of turmoil in the Gas Planet's heart. However, as soon as the threat of destruction had emerged, it dissipated as the GAF ship took the holds place in the centre, allowing the treasure chest to float innocently away for the Bounty to collect.

Kirk Sandblaster's dumb luck had struck again.

14

Now that the Gas Planet had a GAF wreckage at its core, the treasure hold was now flung far out of its orbit and free to float in the big mystery of deep space. If it had thoughts, which of course it hadn't but stick with us here, then it would consider the magnitude of possibilities it now had at its disposal. It would think of all the exotic planets it could fly past, observing it from a deity-like level of perspective. It could encounter strange life-forms, as they flew past it and knew nothing of what it contained. It could just be a simple, unidentified treasure hold, without any of the pressures that came with being a planets nucleus and containing lots and lots of fortune.

Unfortunately for the treasure hold, which definitely wasn't sentient, Kirk Sandblaster and his Zaarian sidekick Xlaar knew it contained treasure, so during its few fleeting moments of independence, it found itself grabbed by the four beefy arms of the Bounty's co-pilot.

On board, Sandblaster was celebrating. Once again he had defied the perils the galaxy threw at him, past treacherous gamblers, mega-suns and hostile bar members. Right now, Cartereli ale in hand and feet aloft, he felt pretty good. Everything was coming up Sandblaster.

Once Xlaar was back on the ship, treasure hold safely stored away in the Bounty's hull, he met up with the utterly chillaxed Sandblaster.

"So... coming to open it?"

Sandblaster dismissed this notion with a flouncy wave of his hand. He had seen many treasures, and another one could surely wait. Right now he just wanted to bask in the moment, in the cool, blinding glow of the Dark Quadrant's mega-sun.

"Seriously. We're not opening it?"

"These things can wait."

Xlaar wasn't in the mood for waiting though. He towered over Sandblaster while he was in full recline and gave him the best stern, four-eyed grimace he could muster.

"I didn't risk my life for 'wait'." He growled.

This was disappointing for Sandblaster. He usually enjoyed the post-adventure relax. It was almost a tradition for him. Sit back, drink a beverage, maybe eat a sandwich and just let yourself go limp. In many ways, it was the best part of an adventure.

"I'll cut you a deal. Let's leave the Dark Quadrant, get to some safe haven and we'll open it there."

"Why can't we..."

"Because this is a moment we should cherish Xlaar!" Sandblaster cried as he leapt from his seat, arms gesticulating wildly. "This is the time we revel in our achievement! We feel the zest of our exploits run through our veins. Why spoil it by running to the end?"

The human had a point. Therefore, Xlaar got behind the controls of the Bounty and prepared to set the sploders to Full. Tinkering with the controls, he couldn't help turning to the strange, excitable comrade of his.

"You know what Sandblaster? I think this may be the beginning of a beautiful relationship."

Sandblaster didn't need to respond. He had a bottle in hand and an arm to raise it. When it came to real men, sometimes that was all you needed to do.

And so the Bounty powered up and blasted its way through the black void that guarded the Dark Quadrant's ginormous sun. Back into a world they knew, with the haul they set out to find.

As Sandblaster said, everything was coming up...

"What then?" The Ghurians cried. Their patience was running thin, especially now the treasure was found.

Before Navi could continue with the tale, Sandblaster popped him off with a jab of his finger.

"I'll field this one Navi!" Sandblaster bellowed, puffing out his chest and preparing his best narrator voice. In the back, Xlaar managed to find a music headset and set it to the Caterwauling Sounds of ROBO-CY-MECH's Finest Droids. Ear-charring music, but far superior to the grandiose oration of Kirk Sandblaster.

Alas, Xlaar only found *one* music headset, and so was doomed to the mono tones of his ship-mate.

So there we were, gliding through the deep darkness of the nastiest bit of space you ever did see. Not that you could see it, because it was unseeable. Total black, darkness. Blacker than the soul of the most evil thing you ever encountered in all your years of space travel.

Yes, it was *that* dark. Bleak, even.

But the visual majesty of the Dark Quadrant isn't important right now. What is, is that I, Kirk Sandblaster, was traversing the treacle tart of space like a fine wine traversing man's gullet. Winding, alone, enveloped in mystery. Not even the assistance of my four-armed friend, Xlaar, could help.

We were on a fast road to nowhere, and had no idea where the exit turn was.

As it happened, it was a mere thousand or so miles away. Which took minutes. But those minutes lasted a lifetime... *of minutes*.

I'll be honest with you, like the computer said I was feeling pretty good. Not quite at the peak of my goodness, that would come later, but I was on the rise. When it comes to adventuring, treasure-hunting is only second to saving maidens, overthrowing villains, saving republics and maybe, just maybe, halting the utter destruction of everything.

In summary, it's pretty Top Tetra.

All I had planned was a sunny planet with cold drinks, large feasts and maybe a lovely female type to compliment, and inform that I respect her feminine ways. If Kirk Sandblaster is one thing, he's a feminist. I totally respect the lady types and their finery. But that was the future, and I was in the now. The now which had a hold full of unknown goodies and a four-armed friend ready to share it all with.

Then you came along...

We had just left the void, sploders pushing us fast through space like a rat out of a cannon. I guess at that point we had rolled all our dice and pushed our luck to the limit as the first thing we encountered was your nefarious vessel.

It took some mighty fine commanding on my half to get Xlaar to steer out your way. But it was too late, you'd seen us and fancied us for swag. I should have pushed on, ran forward and never looked back. But by then I was pretty concussed from falling to the floor with all the wild flailing of the ship and also the celebratory beverages I had consumed. We were in a chase scenario now, and there was no turning back.

Was it an ambush? Or a Mea Culpa on my part? Only history will say, and maybe the victor, but all I'll say now is that we're here and you're there and the treasure is in our hold and the smell of battle is in our nostrils.

"And so," Sandblaster finished up, "this is the now. The present. The past is gone and the future is foggy, much like the Dark Quadrant itself. Well, until you get past the whole void and then encounter that really large and bright sun. It's very nice, you should see it sometime."

"Finished?" The Ghurians asked. Xlaar was hoping he had as he made his way back to the cockpit, the ROBO-CY-MECH music less tolerable than he thought.

"I never finish you Ghurian sivs. Kirk Sandblaster is always in forward motion, like a rolling stone. But seriously, check out the Dark Quadrant. It is dandy stuff."

Sandblaster winked at Xlaar. He was hoping that not only would the Ghurian's take the bait, but that they also lacked tint on their cockpit windows.

"We not dumb!" Was their response.

"Darn." Sandblaster whispered.

"Story over now! We. Want. Treasure!"

Sandblaster took a deep breath and furrowed his brow as he leaned toward the communication speaker. Now was the time to go Full Sandblaster.

"Do your worst..."

"We already did!"

Sandblaster didn't expect this response. He was about to consult Xlaar when, suddenly, they both had a moment of clarity and dinged to what the Ghurians were talking about.

Heading straight for them were the two Xdian Trailblazer Missiles they had conveniently forgotten about. And they were no longer in a position to be overlooked, ignored or even dodged.

All Sandblaster and Xlaar could do was hold on, and hope there'd be no permanent damage...

Xdian's, it should be noted, while absolutely dumb to an almost impressive degree, are *very* handy with blunt instruments. So handy in fact, that when it comes to advanced weaponry, they're just so stupid enough to be able to re-arm it again.

Not to a lethal degree, of course. Martian technology is far too advanced for that sort of re-adjustment. But the wonders that can be done with a few sharp blows from a heavy instrument and some left over cillinium. It can bluntly remove any sort of safety measures in place, and leave you with something that can pack enough of a punch for you to wake up and wonder where the week went.

They hammered everything from laser pistols, which left a nasty mark, to "Boomers" which could rock a small district and maybe dislodge a few mid-sized trinkets. But their Trailblazer Missiles were their main export. Designed to disable spacecraft, with a little bit of Xdian denting they maintain their impressive speed while also adding a blind, explodey quality when making contact. All semblance of subtlety is removed, replaced by a pretty little BANG.

A pretty little BANG which Kirk Sandblaster and Xlaar had just experienced themselves. From the outside, it would indeed have looked quite spectacular, all burning flares and explosive dynamics and just all-round awe-inspiring visuals. However, it was all show and no strength, creating little more than a nasty bump on the Bounty.

No, the real damage was inside, as Sandblaster and Xlaar were finding out. Due to the destabiliser aspects of the Trailblazer's original design, the blast sent a shockwave through the ships computer systems and caused much sparking of electricity and flashes of all-round nastiness. While Sandblaster was flung far from the scene of technological devastation, Xlaar was not so lucky. He found one of his heads flying straight into the control console, and a rogue ZAP of current hit him straight in the eye. Now hopefully none of you have ever had a ZAP of current from a mid-level space ship hit you in the eye, but put it this way: it doesn't end well, and your winking days are well and truly over.

Xlaar roared in pain and clutched his now-blind peeper. The Zaarian had never felt so much pain, and despite all efforts to retain some sort of tough exterior, all he managed to do was not smash the ship apart in rage.

Sandblaster saw his comrade in pain, and rushed to help.

"What happened? Was it your eye?"

Xlaar glared and removed his hands exposing his blitzed optic. It was definitely beyond repair, and Sandblaster's efforts at sensitivity extended to not vomiting. He reared back with a disgusted look and then a fake smile.

"At least you have another 3?"

Xlaar grabbed him by the collar and smashed him against the roof of Bounty's cockpit.

"You want to lose a glatting eye?" He roared in dual-voice.

"We'll buy you a new one! It'll be super-duper! Full of whizz and bang and possibly lasers."

Xlaar roared again and threw Sandblaster to one side. The dumb human meant well, but he had no time for putting up with his spiel. All that was on Xlaar's mind was vengeance, pure and nasty. The Bounty had weapons and he planned to use it. Implementing his own brand of brute force, he pummelled the controls back into some sort of working shape and started punching in the orders.

Both barrels. Full pelt. Right at the Ghurian ship.

The Ghurian's, given their distinct lack of skill in these scenarios, were too busy congratulating themselves on a direct hit to perform any sort of follow up. Instead they remained seated behind the stationary Bounty, seemingly content to let them make their move.

And it was quite the move. Xlaar spun the ship around, putting Sandblaster to the floor again where he was thinking of actually staying rather than get up, and took aim. The blasters wouldn't cause the Ghurians as much damage as they had taken, but it would give them a shock and make Xlaar feel better.

With a battle cry he fired, and the Ghurian ship felt the full force of his righteous anger. The blaster hit it hard, shaking around and actually causing one accidental fatality. One Ghurian was searching for more mind-spirits, which were located next to their ships air lock. When the Bounty's missile hit, the air lock happened to open and the Ghurian stumbled out due to the impact. His final thoughts, which no-one would ever hear or know, were "why did we put a storage cupboard there?"

While Xlaar was happy pelting the Ghurian's with all the firepower he could muster, Sandblaster had other ideas. He crawled across the floor and dragged himself beside Xlaar, to where the sploder controls were. Without Xlaar noticing, he managed to turn them back on and into position for a full reversal. The first the Zaarian noticed of it was when his target was getting smaller.

"What are you doing?"

"What I planned all along..." Sandblaster replied, picking himself up.

The Ghurian's were stumped at the sudden change of tact, and kept to their game-plan of pursuing the Bounty. Soon the chase was back on, with Sandblaster spinning his ship into a more visually pleasing direction.

"But now we can't see them to shoot!" Xlaar protested, but Sandblaster wasn't listening. Maybe it was because he was so focussed on his plan, maybe it was because he didn't want to play his trump card too soon. But more likely was the fact that the ear Xlaar was shouting into had gone a bit deaf thanks to all the explosions.

As the Ghurian ship powered behind them, desperate to catch up, Sandblaster threw the Bounty forward. He checked the co-ordinates of their location, and the results were exactly what he was hoping for. In that moment, he held his breath and prepared himself.

"Xlaar?"

"What?"

Sandblaster didn't say anything, he just smiled.

With the force of his palm, Sandblaster hit the console and suddenly put the Bounty's systems offline. No sploders, no warp drive, nothing. Just the gravitational pull of empty space. A pull that, as always, made the ship drift forcefully out of its trajectory.

A trajectory, which was heading straight back into the Haken Belt.

As the Bounty fell softly in space, the Ghurian ship flew right past. They were going so fast, that any attempt to brake would still mean some serious continuing forward motion. The Ghurian's just looked confused as the Bounty peacefully moved away from where they were chasing it, and looked up to see themselves go front-first into a rather large, and unforgiving, asteroid.

As the stunned Xlaar watched the Ghurian ship blow up into a few thousand tiny pieces, Sandblaster took back his rightful position in his favourite chair.

"You see Xlaar," Sandblaster said, turning to his co-pilot with a sense of triumph and pointing to his head, "not just a hat rack..."

"No. But you never wear hats."

Suddenly Sandblaster turned toward the deep darkness of spaced and stared out bitterly, as if a thousand bad memories hit him at once. "And I never will, not after what they did to my Father..."

But that was a story for another time.

Instead, in the now Xlaar looked at Sandblaster. He had a feeling he knew the answer to the question he was going to ask, for some reason it was almost a foregone conclusion after everything they had been through, but he asked anyway.

"You planned this?"

Naturally, Sandblaster had. He knew that once leaving the Dark Quadrant and intercepting the Ghurian ship and entering a chase, they would soon be in the Haken Belt again. All he needed was a ruse, and Navi had provided them with the story of how they came to be here. After that, it was a simple case of letting their ships get close enough for enacting the final part of his plan.

Of course, he hadn't figured in all the kabooms and blinding of his co-pilot. But such was the spirit of adventure.

Now all that was left was the little matter of the treasure, and celebrating the end of this particular tale to tell. With a glint in his eye, Sandblaster patched in some directions, and leaned back in his chair.

16

Back in the relative safety of the Dilure Quadrant, the bruised and battered, and in the case of Xlaar, blinded crew of the Bounty were ready to call the whole thing a day. Although depending on the planet you were on, that day could have lasted mere minutes or a life-time.

In Xlaar's mind, he felt it was the latter. Definitely the latter.

They had made port in the neutral, mostly desolate planet of Rettaria Minor. While the atmosphere there was rather breathable, it had never really spawned life nor a booming industry due to the more popular destination of Rettaria Major. Not that life had spawned there either, it was just better for commerce.

Minor was home to a few local peddlers and stubborn settlers who preferred the "unique, under-rated" aspect of the planet. They liked its small size, and local feel, and the fact it was better than "those folk over on Rettaria Major, with their hoity-toity ways."

Once they had landed, the first place they went to was a Medi-Officer. Alas, the resident professional was less than properly trained, and almost balked at the sight of Sandblaster's bruised body. When it came to Xlaar's eye, he actually fainted.

After a few moments of striking the doctor to wake him up, he saw to the Bounty's crew the best he could. He prescribed self-medication to Sandblaster, who started right away on another Cartereli, and offered his best medical supplies to Xlaar.

In the form of a rather dashing eye-patch.

"It makes you look dangerous!" Sandblaster assured his hefty friend.

"It makes me look like an idiot."

"A *dangerous* idiot."

After going back to the doctor for the concussion he had just received from Xlaar, Sandblaster made his way to the nearest drinkery.

There, the two beings rested and went over the whole quest. It wasn't the best quest Sandblaster had ever been on; in fact he rated it merely "acceptable", but it was a good way to get Xlaar into his groove.

"This is only the start of things Xlaar, good buddy." Sandblaster toasted with aplomb. "From here on in, things are about to get interesting."

Xlaar didn't like the sound of that.

Still, it had been exciting. Sandblaster's reckless nature and general love of the game, rather than any depraved reasons, was both admirable and thrilling. If he was truly honest with himself, Xlaar would say that his time spent at Space Station Hull had made him believe that he'd never see the buzz of space action again. For those pilots who waited there, the best they could get was a nice courier job that may see them get raided now and again.

But with Sandblaster, they had not only been raided and tricked; they had discovered a whole new solar system and found treasure.

Then it struck Xlaar.

"The treasure!"

"What about it?"

"I think we should open it."

Sandblaster just shrugged, he was sufficiently celebrated now anyway. With a hop and a skip, mainly from him, they returned to the Bounty to collect their find.

In a small desert on the outskirts of a Rettaria settlement, Sandblaster and Xlaar carried the treasure hold that had been their goal since the beginning. In actuality, Xlaar did most of the carrying, while Sandblaster did his best pointing and directing. He was good at that.

The Rettaria deserts were perfect for peaceful moments of lone activity. Why, just on their wander to a more isolated part they had seen young lovers scamper around, lonely folk scampering with their ocular devices, and some curious robots that were best left alone. However, a few miles away from where they were based, they found a place to settle and open up the hold.

"Right. This'll take much cunning, a lot of thinking, and nimble hands to open this..."

With the full force of all four of his mitts, Xlaar slammed the hold so hard that its door snapped open an inch.

Slowly, both beings opened the door to the hold and peered inside.

It was empty, save for a little note. Sandblaster picked it up and read it.

"'Ha! Jokes on you suckers! We stole all the Tetras for our own retirement fund. Signed, the Tetra Bank Couriers.'"

Holding the note, Sandblaster afforded himself a little chuckle at the chutzpah of those who had raided their own hold. It was so out-there, he wondered why he never became a courier and done the same thing himself. He would have been a Tetrilionnairre by now. Even though actually, he was.

For Xlaar though, it was astonishing. All he could was fall to his knees and stare into the empty hold. All the effort he had put in, the things he'd been through, the eye he lost, for a jape.

"Well, looks like the joke's on us dear friend! Guess the Tetras are on me instead."

Xlaar didn't respond. He couldn't. He was stunned.

"Look at it this way, it means you get to spend more time with me to venture into the unknown!"

And with that, Xlaar screamed into the desert, distracting couples, gawkers and robots alike.

Back at the Bounty, Xlaar had settled down. Well not completely, but enough to not want to throw himself into the nearest sun and join his ancestors in the Zaarian afterlife, which by all accounts was rather nice. Waterfalls and epic battles nice, the finest way for a warrior to spend eternity.

But no, instead he sulked and thought about his lost eye. It was still very sour and stung a lot, but a few dozen of Sandblaster's ales had made it go away a bit. In fact, it made him feel a bit woozy, and also a tad emotional.

"I can't believe this, is what I've become." Xlaar said, motioning to the battered ship he was sat in on the wasteland planet they had docked.

Sandblaster was less morose and more in spirit with the whole thing. He looked to his co-pilot and did his best heroic pose.

"Lift those spirits soldier, because this is just the start of a beautiful relationship."

"Says who?"

"Says me! And I say a lot."

Xlaar definitely knew that.

"Now see here, you may feel a little hard done by now, but dagnabbit you had fun! Right?"

He couldn't deny it. The whole thing *had* been quite fun.

"Yes we've got no real treasure, but we've acquired the best treasure of all."

Xlaar knew that whatever was coming next, it was going to be cheesy. He steeled himself for it.

"We have the treasure, of friendship."

He nearly vomited. Sandblaster continued as he looked out of the Bounty's window wisely.

"Who knows what the future holds? I certainly don't. And I don't want to! All I want is the buzz of a quest, the thrill of a journey, a few fine beverages and eats along the way and most of all?"

Xlaar looked at the frantic human who had dragged him into this whole mess.

"A comrade to experience it all with."

Sandblaster offered his hand, and for a moment Xlaar just looked at it. Then, with his emotions welling up, he grabbed it with all four of his mighty hands and shook so hard that Sandblaster was lifted in the air and once again, brained on the roof.

"Blarney cake." Sandblaster said in his concussed state.

After a moment of recovery, both beings settled into their cockpit seats and powered up the Bounty. They bid farewell to the rather rubbish planet of Rettaria Minor, you could really see why Major was the superior location, and all they left behind of their visit was one empty hold and the mocking note left inside.

As Xlaar took command of the flight controls, Sandblaster pieced together a sandwich, took a bite, and nodded as he saw space wrap around his ship and the stars glitter as they flew past.

"So, where to now?" Xlaar asked.

Sandblaster considered this for a moment, and then smiled.

"Well I do recall we've come across a whole new Quadrant to explore. Think there'll be any treasure in there?"

"As long as it doesn't have any stupid notes in it."

Both men laughed, this time Sandblaster only having a minor heart attack at the sound of Xlaar's shrill guffaws. Sandblaster gave the word, Xlaar entered in the co-ordinates to take them to the Dark Quadrant, and Navi complied.

With a shining streak, the Bounty flew into the beautiful mystery of space. And all the adventure that awaited.

Kirk Sandblaster WILL return in...

Kirk Sandblaster & the Ice Pirates of Llurr!

Oli Jacobs continues to write books, drink ale, and eat curry. You can tweet him at @OliJacobsAuthor or read his work at http://www.DoYouLikeWords.com

As always, he hopes you enjoy

Printed in Great Britain
by Amazon